PATRICIA E. CANTERBURY

THE SECRET OF
ST. GABRIEL'S TOWER

a Poplar Cove Mystery

♠

ReGeJe Press
Sacramento, California

For information, address ReGeJe Press, P O Box 293442 Sacramento, CA
95829, (916)681-5557

ISBN 0-9639147-6-6

♠

First edition: September 1998
10 9 8 7 6 5 4 3 2 1

Cover art: Jamie Coudright

To my husband, Richard, for identifying the girls and for his unquestionable belief that the book would be published.

To the Sunday ZICA Creative Arts and Literary Guild members who encouraged me to expand the short story, which introduced The Triplets, to a full-length novel.

Thanks, Ethel Mack Ballard, Jacqueline Turner Banks, Terris McMahon Grimes, Geri Spencer Hunter and the late Ceola Jackson for helping me give the girls' voices. And to Maggie Lean who allowed us to use her home for our readings, critique and discussions every Sunday and for her unabashed enthusiasm in the girls' lives, Thanks.

A special thanks to Sara Paretsky for her support and encouragement to develop a series around the girls.

And thanks to Joseph Cantrell, Sr., for his very generous support.

CHAPTER 1

"Don't ya have somethin' to do?" Ruthie Joan asked her little sister, Hattie. The little girl, standing just inside their parent's bedroom door, with her dirty face smudged and sweaty from hard play, didn't reply. Hattie smiled as she continued to watch her older sister's secret ritual. Ruthie Joan turned back to the cracked mirror. She continued to study her tear-streaked dark brown face as she sat at their mother's dressing table. She put dark red lipstick on her full lips and then pinched her cheeks to bring out a hint of color to her face. She wiped her tear-swollen eyes.

"Why are ya crying? Are ya crying 'cuz ma ain't home? Why are you in ma and pa's room? Why ain't you in our room? Are you using ma's lipstick again? Put some on me," Hattie demanded as she hitched her too-big pants over her bony butt and sat down in the doorway.

Suppressing a sob and blowing her nose on a threadbare white handkerchief, Ruthie Joan said, "I ain't crying. And you can't wear ma's stuff. Least not while you're dirty and wearing

The Secret of St. Gabriel's Tower

Johnny's old hand-me-down pants. Where's the dress I ironed for you?"

"It's too pretty to wear in the garden."

"You might as well wear nice things while you got 'em. Now go outside and help the boys."

"Ya shouldn't cry. Ya should come out and play with me."

"Maybe I'll play with you tomorrow. Remember how we've been practicin' to say you instead of ya?"

"Uh huh."

"Don't forget. Manner is very important. Ma'll be home soon, and she's gonna need me today."

"Ma's coming home soon? Is that why ya... uh you, putting on ma's stuff? You look real pretty Ruthie Joan. You smell nice too. You're wearing ma's perfume? I like the way it smells—like roses. Are you goin' somewhere? Can I come with you? Please, please, please? Take me with you," Hattie begged, jumping up quickly and hopping up and down, the reflection of her small face popping in and out of the mirror.

"I'm not going no where. I just want to look nice. You should always try to look nice. You can wear ma's stuff when you're grown up. Now you go outside, like I said, and help them boys in the garden. Ma's gonna want fresh vegetables for the soup." Ruthie Joan patted Hattie on her bottom and pushed her gently out of their parents' room.

Sitting on the padded floral bench in front of the dresser for another five minutes, Ruthie Joan spoke aloud to her reflection."

"Ruthie Joan, you're gonna die right here in Poplar Cove without going no where. With the new baby coming, Ma's going to need your help. Might as well help with brothers and sisters 'cuz nobody's ever gonna marry you and take you away from here. You gonna be taking care of your brothers and sisters til you're an old maid." Tears once again filled her light brown eyes and rolled down her lightly powdered cheeks. "And it's all 'cuz of this here polio."

Placing the lipstick and perfume back in it's normal place, she picked up a green satin ribbon lying across a China music box and tied it around one loose dark brown curl. Fluffing the ribbon in her hair, Ruthie Joan looked around the tiny bedroom that was nearly twice the size of the space she shared with Hattie. She'd memorized every inch: the large brass double bed that took up most of the room, the small oak dresser, the floral bench and the oak wardrobe her mother had brought before Teddy, the oldest, was born. Getting up slowly, she smoothed the corner of the peach colored chenille bedspread, brushing away imaginary dust where Hattie had placed her hands.

As she walked carefully past the oak dresser, she accidentally knocked her leg braces against it.

"Oh no, did I scratch it?" She bent over and inspected the tiny nick an inch above the floor. "No one'll notice it," she said to herself, limping out of the room and shutting the door behind her.

She glanced at the *Repeater* clock above the fireplace; and, smoothing wrinkles from her freshly ironed green and white gingham dress, Ruthie Joan opened the front door. Walking as quietly as her braces allowed, she headed down the dirt road toward Old Mill Road.

Moments later a black 1910 Ford coupe stopped next to where she stood catching her breath in the shade of a large pine tree. The driver, a brown-skinned young man dressed in a new-looking tan linen vested suit, leaned toward the passenger's window, tipped his tan cap, and said. "Hi. I ain't seen you at TriCove high. Are you new to this area?"

Stammering and blushing, Ruthie Joan limped closer to the passenger's side of the car. "No, I . . . I don't go to TriCove High."

"Are you new to Poplar Cove?"

"Uh uh."

Quickly glancing at the silver crucifix resting at her throat, he continued, "oh, ya must go to St. Catherine's, over near Weed. Most of the Catholic girls go there. I'm going to Marshall. Want to come with me?" he asked, opening the door.

I'm not supposed t' go no where with strangers, she thought. Ma'd be real mad if I got in this here car. But she'll be home in an hour or so. The kids'll be okay. Nobody'd even miss me.

"Well are ya comin' or are just gonna stand there starin' at me?" The young man asked, with a smile.

"I hafta be back home by 5:00. What time is it now?"

He took out a pocket watch and glanced at it before answering. "Almost noon," he answered, putting the watch back in his vest pocket.

"Okay." Ma'll be home in an hour. She'll just have to be mad, when she finds out I went for this ride, Ruthie Joan mused. Besides, nothing's gonna happen. She struggled getting into the car, but he didn't seem to notice. "The kids can play til Ma returns." She realized she'd said the words out loud as she fell against the young man while reaching for her fallen hair ribbon. "Sorry," she said, again blushing deeply and tying the ribbon tighter on her curls.

"I ain't fraid of polio like some. We could have fun. What kids were you talkin' about?"

"Oh, just my little sister and four little brothers. They're playing out back." She looked back toward her house nestled in the redwoods. She could still hear the high, childish squeals of her siblings' summer fun.

"What kind of fun?" she asked, looking past the young man to a clearing where her brother Teddy plowed the back acre of the Shaw's farm. Teddy, intent on plowing, didn't look up as his sister rode down Old Mill Road with her new friend. She smiled, the answer to her question didn't matter. "Yeah, we can have fun."

♠

"What are we going to do for fun this summer?" Amber asked, squinting at the last page of her worn history book. She and her two closest friends, Jessica Johnson and Robyn Jones, sat in the cat's paw grass behind Lost Whale Tavern overlooking the Pacific Ocean.

"I don't know. What do you want to do?" Robyn asked. "I know I don't want to sit around the house baby sitting my little brothers. Adam's barely walking; and he already wants to come everywhere with me. It's like I have three shadows when he and Junior tag along."

"The boys are fun. They're no trouble at all," Jessica said, pulling her father's battered fedora further down over her already red and freckled face.

"You just say that 'cuz you don't live with 'em all the time."

"Maybe. I remember Jimmy Wil let me follow him around all the time. Sometimes I wish he wasn't away at school." Jessica grinned as she pictured her older brother. "Mom and Dad used to worry about me. Said I'd turn out to be a tomboy. But I didn't." She enunciated each word slowly, her noticeable lisp held momentarily in check.

"Speaking of tomboys, I know something exciting we could do to get the summer started just right," Amber said, her foghorn voice echoing in the air as she absent-mindedly picked at a scab on her left knee. Her long, dark brown curly hair blew into her face, causing her to squint more than usual.

"What?" Jessica and Robyn asked in unison.

"We could paint our names on the Main Square water tower tomorrow night."

"What? Are you crazy? We'd get caught," Jessica said. She turned around to face the tiny colored town of Poplar Cove. Pointing in the direction of the tower she said, "You can see the Main Square tower from way over here. It's the tallest thing in town."

"That's right. You can see it from the highway. It's the symbol of our town. Why should the boys from Grant's Cove, who don't even live here, be the only ones to climb it?" Amber retorted.

The Secret of St. Gabriel's Tower

"But . . . but they're the only ones who *do*. It's part of graduation. We won't be graduating from high school for six more years!" Robyn answered.

Getting up and turning around, Amber stared in the direction of town. "I can't see anything. It's too hazy, but I know it's there. You don't hear about graduating Grant's Cove girls climbing the tower. We'll be 'ladies' by then and our mothers won't let us do it."

"Our Mom's, *yours* included, won't let us climb the tower *now*. You know they definitely won't let us in six years. Amber, you need glasses. It's not foggy or hazy out here," Jessica teased.

"I do not need glasses. I'm not going to wear any thick, black ugly old things like Miss Beauregard. I'm squinting 'cuz I'm not tall like you and Robyn. You can see farther than me. Besides, we were talking about the watertower." Amber sat down on the high dry grass. She picked up a skinny piece of driftwood and started to draw a crude picture of the watertower on the only bare spot within yards.

"What's that you're drawing?" Robyn asked, moving closer to patch of earth with Amber's artwork.

"The watertower. If we climbed up on this side near Carver Street, no one will see us. We'll paint our names on it; and, when everyone wakes up Saturday morning, they'll know that we beat the boys," she said, a cat-like smile on her olive face.

"When are we going to do this?" Robyn asked. "The boys will be up there tomorrow night. Tonight mama's helping me sew my dress for next Sunday's Mass."

"We could do it tonight, after ten. You'll be finished. All of us should be finished with our chores by then."

"We are also going to St. Gabriel's for my birthday celebration aren't we?" Robyn asked.

"Of course. We always spend our birthdays in St. Gabriel's. You've asked the same question every day this week. What's so important about this birthday?" Jessica teased.

"Nothing. Besides, I don't know if mama will let me go back out. We have to get up early for school tomorrow."

12

"We only have one more day. Besides, Mrs. Blake's already told us that the American history test is the last thing we're doing in the sixth grade. We've studied ourselves silly. We know the answers. We can be a little sleepy and still get 'A's.'"

"Yes. We'll still get 'A's,'" Robyn added.

"So, are we going to climb to the top of the tower?"

"Yes," the other two replied.

♠

"Ruthie Joan? Ruthie, honey, Mama's home. Hattie, where's Ruthie Joan?" Mrs. Freeman asked, taking off her blue felt hat and ever present coat. She owned six coats, more than anyone in Poplar Cove. Even Mrs. Anderson, with all her furs, didn't own as many full-length coats as Mrs. Freeman. She wore them rain or shine, hot or cold, to church, to her occasional day job in Marshall, even during the rare times when she had a minute to herself, just to gossip with neighbors. Today she wore a blue and black lightweight cotton plaid coat and white lace gloves.

"*Dent'* no. I ain't seen her for a long time," seven year old Hattie said as she rubbed her runny nose with the back of her dirty hand and onto the same too-big pants she'd worn for two days.

"Whatcha mean you don't know?" Mrs. Freeman asked, kissing her on the only clean space on her youngest daughter's dirty face.

"I ain't seen her. She left. She and Teddy had a fight. She's so pretty. Mama, ain't I pretty like Ruthie Joan?"

"Yes, you're mama's pretty little girl," Mrs. Freeman replied, looking around the small house as if Ruthie Joan would appear from behind the sofa. "You said that Ruthie Joan left? Where'd she go? And where is Teddy? Why didn't Ruthie Joan comb your hair? Look at you, your braids done all come out. Where's Teddy? Where'd they go?"

The Secret of St. Gabriel's Tower

"Teddy's out back. He still got the piece by Mrs. Shaw t' work. Whatcha bring me?"

"Go out back and pump some water in the basin over there," she said, pointing to the white enameled basin on the corner of the kitchen table. "And wash your face. Looks like you haven't washed up proper in days. Then I'll show you what I brung all you kids. Git," Mrs. Freeman said, patting Hattie on her bottom. She eased off her "Sunday go to meeting shoes." Carefully wrapping the black patent leather shoes in a gunnysack, which she took out of her large black handbag, she sat down heavily on the worn horsehair sofa, knocking off a starched white antimacassar onto the bright, yet dirty, yellow linoleum floor. Rubbing her tired sore feet, she eased back onto the sofa. Four little boys, ages four, six, eight and ten, rushed into the house and enveloped her in hugs and dirty wet kisses before she settled back on the sofa.

"Boys..., boys..., go find Hattie. Wash your faces," Mrs. Freeman said, giving each boy a return hug and kiss.

"But Ma."

"And them hands! My Goodness, look at you," she said, getting up slowly her stomach already showing, the signs of another child. "Come here, Ralphie," she said, inspecting the slightly matted head of the four year old. "You'd think that Ruthie Joan wasn't lookin' after you. Where is that girl?"

♠

"Mother, can I go over to Jessica's after dinner?" Amber asked, setting three places on the dining room table.

"After dinner? Don't you see enough of her at school? Haven't you two been together all day? Don't you need to study? There's only one more day of school, and then you two have the entire summer."

"But, Mother."

14

"But mother what?" Mable Louise asked, softly looking up from the lamb stew she'd been stirring on the Wedgewood stove.

"I... um... I have one of her papers by mistake."

"I wish the Johnsons' would get a telephone. You could call her, and she could come over here and get it. I guess it's okay, but don't stay out too late."

"Thanks, mother, besides nobody's going to bother me. I'll be right back," Amber said, hiding her crossed fingers behind her back.

♠

"Mama, can I go over to Amber's?" Robyn asked, placing the sheet music for *Scott Joplin's* THE ENTERTAINER, on the family's upright Eilers piano.

"You still have to practice your piano lesson instead of wasting time on that brothel music," Ethelene Jones said, putting the sheet music away and placing two classical pieces in its place. "Then we're going to work on your dress for Sunday. Look at you. I can't believe that you want to walk around all day in your father's old overalls. You look like an orphan. I'll be lucky to get you to wear a dress on Sunday."

Robyn watched her mother walk out of the parlor and into the kitchen.

"Then can I go see Amber?"

"Don't you see enough of each other at school? I don't want you wandering all over town," Ethelene called, from the kitchen.

"Up," fourteen-month old Adam said, pulling at his sister's torn overall pant leg.

"Mama, Adam's disturbing me."

"Up." Adam repeated, holding his chubby brown arms in the air.

15

The Secret of St. Gabriel's Tower

"Were twain?" three-year-old Junior asked, walking into the parlor after Adam, a red, wooden, caboose held tightly in his plump left hand.

"Adam were twain?"

"Mama, Junior's in here. I can't practice with the boys in here, Mama."

"I heard you the first time, Robyn. There's no need to shout. You weren't raised in a barn. You shouldn't let the boys bother you. Keep practicing. Hand me that sheet music I just gave you," Ethelene said. She came back from the kitchen and looked over the chords for Mozart's Sonata in C major. "Let's try again. Put your fingers here. That's better. Keep practicing, we have an hour before supper. Set the table after you finish that piece. You have to know the classics before you can play modern music well. Come on boys, leave your sister alone. You can come into the kitchen and help me cook. Junior take that caboose out of your mouth." She took the boys by the hand and walked them out of the parlor.

"Robyn you should be helping your mother instead of being a burden. You know that she has her hands full with the boys," Homer Senior said, walking into the parlor, a copy of the Poplar Cove Weekly tucked under his arm.

"Daddy, can I go over to Amber's after supper?"

"What did your mother say?"

"She didn't answer."

"You'll have to ask her again. Wait until the boys are in bed. I don't want them following you all over town, *if* you go out."

"I'll read them a story after supper, *Treasure Islands*. It's so long it always puts them to sleep. Then I'll ask Mama."

"That'll be nice. Finish your practicing. You're still using the wrong fingering on that piece. Wash up and set the table in a half hour, or you'll be practicing til midnight." He left the room, and she could see through the window that he was outside and lighting one of his cigars.

"Why're Mama and Daddy so worried about me going out at night? They worry more now that I'm eleven than when I was a little kid. It's not like anythin' ever happens here," Robyn said to herself.

♠

"Mom, Dad, can I go over to Robyn's tonight after dinner?" Jessica asked, shelling fresh peas into a dish over the kitchen sink.

"Don't you girls see enough of each other at school? What on earth do you find to talk about all the time? When I was your age I was apprenticing with one of Madame Walker's best students. You didn't find me sitting around all day talking and dreaming of moving pictures," Ruby Sue said, opening the oven door and sticking a long handled fork into the juicy brown skin of a pork roast.

"But Mom, you knew you wanted to be a beautician since you were little. You have your own shop..."

"Which is only open two days a week. I can't help your father build for our future working only two days a week," Ruby Sue interrupted.

"But Mom, you have the only shop for miles around. Women are gonna..."

"Jessica, what'd I tell you about speaking properly. 'Gonna', isn't a word. Say going to."

"Yesth, Ma'ma, going to. Women are going to want to have someone do their hair. I read it in one of them... uh ... in one of the motion picture magazines from New York. It said colored women were going to shops to have their hair pressed by professionals. All the women in the magazine were beautiful. Mom, you could make them even prettier. You're a professional."

"You can stop the sweet talk, JJ. You have to stay home tonight. There is only a day left in the school year. You'll be underfoot all summer. I'll be begging you to go see your friends.

The Secret of St. Gabriel's Tower

You can see Robyn or Amber all you want after tomorrow," Ruby Sue said, with a smile, hugging her tall, thin daughter.

"Ouch."

"Have you gotten sunburned already? It's not even Juneteenth yet, and you're already burned. You don't usually burn til late August. Let me look at you." Ruby Sue led Jessica closer to the bright kitchen lamp sitting on the large oak table. She felt her daughter's forehead. "You don't seem to have a fever. Did you wear a hat as I asked?"

"*Yesth*, Mom, I wore Dad's old grey fedora. Can I go? I promised."

"Promised what?"

"I promised Robyn I'd help her with her homework."

"Uh huh. Whatever it is you two, or should I say three, are cooking up, I want you to stay out of trouble."

"How could we get in trouble? We're just girls in a small quiet, boring town," Jessica replied, her lisp barely surfacing, as she put the last of the shelled peas in a small pot of water.

♠

"Teddy, where's Ruthie Joan? Isn't she with you?" Mrs. Freeman asked her oldest as he walked into the house.

Brushing dust off his overalls and wiping sweat from his face, Teddy hugged his mother; and, walking over to the stove, lifted the top off the steaming pot of vegetable soup.

"Um... Good to have you back, Ma. Supper smells good. I'm starvin'."

"Where's Ruthie Joan?" Mrs. Freeman asked, again.

"I don't know. She's gotta be round somewhere. I been up early working on the old Shaw place for the last coupla days. Mr. Shaw said he'd let me sharecrop his back five acres, the ones close to Old Mill Road. Maybe he'd let us keep it for farmin' then we could use that plot outside to enlarge the house. We're really gonna

18

need more space with the new one coming. Pa's havin' a hard time finding work. We can't have him going to Mt. Shasta ever time things git slow 'round here."

"I know. You're a good son. I'm just worried about Ruthie Joan. It ain't like her not to be here."

"Ma, I can't keep an eye on Ruthie Joan and the little ones and work all day in the fields. I ain't seen her today. Ask Hattie. I been gettin' up before dawn, and I don't get home til near nine. I told Ruthie Joan I'd fix my own supper and lunch. She wasn't doing nothing 'cept moping around. I left her sitting by the window when I left."

"But she shouldn't leave the little ones," his mother said, crying. "I wish I wouldn't cry all the time. This baby's coming too soon. I feel it," she continued, wiping her face with a clean piece of torn flannel.

"Ma, you shouldn't get upset. Hattie's little; she don't have no sense o' time. Ruthie Joan's never left the kids for more than a hour or so. Besides, she can't 've gone far, not with her leg. She might've gone to see Miz. Shaw. She goes over there when the kids get on her nerves or Eli Shaw's not around. You know he don't take kindly to folks in his home. No need to worry 'bout her; nobody's going do nothing to her;" he said, taking the dipper from the wooden bucket on the wash basin and pouring water over his dark curly hair and neck.

CHAPTER 2

"What are you girls doing up there?" Sheriff Brown shouted at the three figures froze in the glare of his and Deputy Blake's flashlights. Staring at the three small figures on the walkabout on the Main Square watertower and motioning for them to come down, he spoke softly to himself, "these Triplets will be the death of me yet."

"Oh oh, we're in for it now," Amber whispered.

"I told you we shouldn't have come up here," Robyn said quietly.

"Come down here, immediately," Sheriff Brown said out loud.

"We're coming, Sheriff Brown." Lisping so hard that her words were barely discernable, Jessica put one foot tentatively on the ladder. "Mom is going to kill me for sure after this."

"You wanted to come as much as we did," Amber said, her nervous voice rivaling the Poplar Cove foghorn. "Robyn, you

The Secret of St. Gabriel's Tower

better go first. I don't want you getting scared and throwing up on us."

"I don't throw up anymore. That only happened when I was a little kid. I haven't thrown up in six months," Robyn protested; but she took a tentative step down the wooden rungs of the Carver Street ladder. The others followed her slowly.

"I should have known. It's the Triplets," Edwain Blake, the new Deputy, said, keeping his flashlight on the descending figures.

"Climbing the water tower may be a rite of passage for the boys from TriCove High, but I must say I *am* surprised at you three," Sheriff Brown said, herding the girls onto the hay wagon he and the Deputy were returning to the train station.

"Why should the big boys have all the fun? We were just writing our names on the tower so they'd know that we could do whatever they did," Amber said.

"And better," Jessica added.

"Your parents can deal with you. Naomi said you girls were the brightest young girls she'd ever taught. What you did tonight isn't very bright. Thank God, I don't have children." Deputy Blake said, mostly to himself, smoothing back an errant strand of coal black hair from his medium brown face.

"You don't have to say anything to Daddy, Sheriff," Amber said, wiping a smudge of blue paint from her cheek with one of her father's cotton handkerchiefs.

"Who's that over there?" Robyn asked, attempting to divert the Sheriff and Deputy. She pointed to a solitary male figure, dressed in a tan suit, hurrying down Abner Bend Road in the direction of the ocean. "Who is that?" she asked again.

"Where?" Amber asked, squinting into the darkness. The Sheriff and Deputy ignored both girls and flashed their lights around the tower searching for more youngsters.

"Nobody, I guess. I thought I saw someone hurrying down the street," Robyn said, holding her left hand over her mouth.

"Are you going to be sick?" Jessica moved away to the far side of the hay wagon and pushed an empty tin bucket in Robyn's direction.

22

"No, I'm not. My stomach's upset," Robyn answered, her light brown eyes filling with tears.

"Don't cry. You know how you break out whenever you cry. Your face was clearing up," Amber said, and handed Robyn a corner of the paint splattered handkerchief to dry her tears.

♠

"Mayor, Mrs. Lincoln, Deputy Blake and I found Amber on the Main Square water tower," Sheriff Brown said, standing in front of the screen door on the Walker's porch. Amber, standing behind him, said nothing.

"Amber?" Mable Louise began.

"Mother, I..."

"Amber come in the house. Mable Louise's eyes never left her daughter as she spoke to the Sheriff. "Thank you, Zachary. We'll take over from here." She opened the door and pulled Amber inside. Tipping his hat to Mable Louise, Sheriff Brown walked back to the hay wagon. Lincoln Walker his face stern said nothing during the Sheriff's brief visit.

Robyn's dark face and Jessica's pale face peered at the door closing behind Amber.

"I can't believe that I've just heard. My daughter writing her name *on* the water tower?" Linc Walker repeated the words over and over as he sat down on the sofa in the parlor, a strong cup of tea cooling on the oak end table at his elbow. He shook his head in disbelief. He got up and poured spirits into the tea and taking a sip, he looked over at his wife, opened and then closed his mouth and returned to the sofa. He stared straight ahead for a few minutes longer then turned toward Mable Louise, who was seated to his left in a wooden straight back chair biting her top lip and waiting for him to continue.

"Mable Louise, perhaps we should send Amber to stay with George and Myrtle over in Marshall Cove for the summer. If she's

23

The Secret of St. Gabriel's Tower

writing her name on private property like some adolescent boy while she's just twelve, what will she going to be doing later?"

"Linc, I'll talk to her. I'll think of something to keep her busy during the summer. She and the other girls are just curious." A fleeting smile crossed her full lips. She brushed back a fallen strand of reddish-brown hair and eased back into her chair, waiting for his response.

"Curious? Shaming me and you in front of the whole town! I'll teach her curious. I need to think. We'll discuss this further tomorrow. I'm going for a walk."

Amber heard the screen door slam and looked out her bedroom window and saw her father walking slowly down Hill Street still talking out loud to himself. Opening her bedroom door and hearing her mother singing softly, she frowned and walked back to the window. Her father continued walking down the street.

♠

"Hello, Sheriff, what brings you out so late? Robyn...?" Ethelene asked, staring at Robyn's tear stained face.

"Mama I'm sorry. I..."

"Sheriff, what happened?" Ethelene repeated, rushing outside. She stepped down the stair and put her arms around her sobbing daughter.

"We found The Triplets on top of the Main Street Tower."

"The tower... Robyn?"

"She's alright. More frightened about getting a spanking then anything else."

"Thank you, Sheriff. Ethelene and I will take care of our daughter," Homer said, taking Robyn's arm and pushing her firmly into the house.

"So that's why you wanted to go out," Sheriff Brown, walking down the steps of the Jones' home, heard Homer say through an open window. He didn't stay to hear Robyn's reply.

"Robyn, what did I tell you earlier about not being a burden to your mother? Look at your mother. You gave her quite a scare. What if the boys had been up? What kind of example are you setting for them? Don't you know you could have gotten hurt? Don't you have anything to say?"

"Mama, Daddy...," was all she could say before cupping her hands over her mouth and running to the water closet to the left of the parlor.

"Now she's going to be up all night being sick, and tomorrow her face will be full of pimples. I don't know what's happened to her. It seems like it was just a few weeks ago that she was a gentle, quiet child. Now she's an eleven-year-old tower climber. What next?" Ethelene said, standing outside the water closet as her daughter heaved on the other side of the door.

"Robyn, open the door and let me come in. We'll talk about your troubles tomorrow. Homer, honey, check on the boys. I'll stay with Robyn for a while. I'll keep her home tomorrow."

"Okay, Lenie, but you coddle that girl too much."

"I know she has to make her own mistakes. I just hope this is the most trouble she has in her life. I'll be up in a minute. I want to make sure she's alright. She's sick and too old to spank, but she has to realize that she's in serious trouble."

"Okay, we'll talk after she's in bed. After I check on the boys, I'm going for a walk."

♠

"Zachary, what a pleasant surprise! Hello, Edwain," Jimmy John said, opening the front door to Sheriff Brown's knock, a fresh cup of coffee in his hand. "What can I do for you?"

"I brought Jessica home."

"JJ? What's she doing with you? Has something happened? Ruby Sue, come out! Something's happened to JJ," Jimmy John

25

said, rushing down the stairs to the hay wagon, spilling coffee and dropping his cup in the rose bush.

"JJ what?" Ruby Sue cried, running from the rear of the house to the front porch.

"No, no, nothing's happened to her. I'm just returning her. Deputy Blake and I caught the Triplets writing their names on the Main Square Tower."

"You what?" Ruby Sue exclaimed, wiping her hands on a white cotton apron sprinkled with bright violets.

"I caught..."

"We heard you. Jessica June Johnson come in this house this minute," Ruby Sue said, standing on the front porch waiting for Jessica to get out of the hay wagon. She watched as her husband rushed to the wagon and cupped Jessica's chin in his hand. He dropped his hand in disgust

"Mom, Dad, I..."

Jimmy John picked up the cup he'd dropped. He shook Sheriff Brown's hand and walked slowly up the stairs. He did not speak.

"Jessica, I won't tell you again. Don't put our business in the street. Come in this house—this minute! Good night, Sheriff, Deputy. Jessica, inside."

"*Yesth*, Mom." Jessica's words were muffled by the heavy oak door closing tightly behind her.

"You're staying home. You cannot see the other Triplets for ... for a week. I don't know what's happened to you. You *used* to be a sweet little girl. You turned eleven and forgot your manners. You're going to the Shop with me tomorrow where I can keep an eye on you."

"But Mom, I have a test."

"I'll have Mrs. Blake give you the test at the shop. I'll press her hair for her. You're to stay away from Robyn and Amber. I don't know what's gotten into you. Go to your room."

"Dad."

"You heard your mother. I'm very disappointed in you. Very disappointed. I don't want you near the other girls."

26

He patted his shirt pockets for matches. Daughters! Ruby Sue and I wanted a daughter so badly, and look at what we got. She's got four times the trouble in her than Jimmy Wil. What are we going to do with her? Jimmy John walked back outside and sat down on the porch swing. Reaching into his breast pocket and he took out and slowly unwrapped a cigar. Biting off the end, he lit it and inhaled deeply. After a few minutes, he tapped ashes from the smoking cigar onto the rose bed. Lincoln Walker walking past didn't look up nor cease mumbling to himself. Jimmy John, also deep in thought, didn't see him as he ground cigar ashes into the rich soil.

♠

"Ruthie Joan's disappeared. She didn't come home last night!" Mrs. Freeman shouted, bursting into the Sheriff's office. Gasping for breath and running her white gloved hands over her lightly powdered face, she continued, "I come back from Marshall Cove yesterday and my youngest girl, Hattie, she tells me that Ruthie Joan's been gone all day. I didn't believe her. But Ruthie Joan didn't come home last night." Pausing for a second, Mrs. Freeman leaned against the Sheriff's desk. Rushing from behind his desk, Deputy Blake helped her to a seat.

"I don't think she run off. I shoulda listened to her. I know sometimes she resents watching the little ones, but Theodore's in Mt. Shasta. You know he's working a few weeks for the Cumberland Logging Company? I've been in Marshall Cove."

"Wait here. I'll get you a cup of water," Deputy Blake interrupted. He handed the full tin cup of water to her before taking a seat on the edge of the desk.

"Thanks," she replied automatically, her face never leaving Sheriff Brown's.

"Uh huh. You've been in Marshall Cove for how long?"

The Secret of St. Gabriel's Tower

"Huh? Oh, I work for Miz Young one day a week while she's gitting over her operation. She took a turn for the worse, and I had to stay three days this time. We don't have no phone; but I told Buddy, that be Buddy Shaw, to tell Teddy and Ruthie Joan that I'd be back on Thursday. That was yesterday. Somebody's took her. I know it. I feel it here." She pointed to her heart. Mrs. Freeman gripped the desk to steady herself. Her face was pale and her eyes wild. "Somebody took her when she was walking. Yes, that's what happened. Somebody saw her and took her."

Pushing some papers and magazines from the only other chair in the station to the floor, Sheriff Brown sat down and took her gloved hand into his massive brown one. He said, "There there, Mary. Take it easy. Have another drink of water. Good."

She looked down at her feet, then from the Sheriff to Deputy Blake. She unconsciously rubbed the lip of the cup spilling some of the water on her gloved hands.

"I don't know where she could be. She couldn't have gone very far. I know she likes to walk to strengthen her legs. But they ain't never gonna be..." Her voice breaking, she took a larger swallow of water.

"She's real shy, you know, 'bout the polio. She never needed no iron lung like some, just the braces. But they came off right before Christmas last year. She was so excited that she wouldn't have to have the braces on at night. She just wears them when she goes outside. She just has a limp now."

"Don't worry, Mary, we'll find her." He called to the night Deputy, "Cal, get a posse and we'll find Ruth Joan. She couldn't go very far. Blake, you take Mrs. Freeman home then come back here. How'd you get here, Mary?"

"Get here? Oh, I brought Teddy's wagon."

"Best thing you can do right now is go home and rest. I'll send Mrs. Wilson over to look in on you. You need to conserve your strength. We'll find Ruthie Joan. Edwain, take the car and hurry back. We'll bring the wagon over in the morning. Cal, go to Mrs. Wilson's and take her over to Mrs. Freeman's. Ring the volunteer fire bell; make sure to pause after the second ring, that'll round up a posse."

Who'd kidnap a crippled girl? I have to agree with Mary, I don't believe that Ruthie Joan's run away, he thought, as he picked up the cup Mrs. Freeman'd used, rinsing it out with hot water from the pot. Maybe I better ring up Constable Greer over in Marshall Cove, he decided as he dried the cup and hung it on the rear door's hook.

Deputy Blake was back in fifteen minutes. "I know Ruthie Joan. She's the only child in Poplar Cove to contract polio. For months after she got the disease parents wouldn't allow their children to swim in the river, and most shut their houses tight all that summer to prevent the disease from coming in the windows," he said to his boss and friend.

"Ruthie Joan is sixteen and in the eighth grade. She lost all those years of school after she got polio. She's a loner and self conscious about her limp."

"Not very grown up even though a lot of girls back home are married by sixteen," Deputy Blake said.

"Married. Poor thing. I don't think her mother would allow her to court even if one of these farm boys could see beyond her limp. It's late but we might find something if we get started right away. If we don't find her tonight we may have to have a second posse out early tomorrow morning. I wonder what's happening to the girls of this town. The Triplets climbing the water tower, I've never heard of girls doing that, ever," Sheriff Brown said, shaking his head. "Now, Ruthie Joan disappearing. I wonder what this world's coming to? Kids! Give me common drunken cowboys any day." He unlocked the rack holding the shotguns and took out two of the four.

Sheriff Brown and Deputy Blake walked outside to meet the posse.

"Cal, you stay here in case Ruthie Joan shows up before we come back. I called Constable Greer to ask around Marshall Cove. If she's been there, someone's bound to have seen her. Let's go find a missing girl."

The Secret of St. Gabriel's Tower

CHAPTER

3

At seven o'clock Saturday morning, Sheriff Brown and Deputy Blake were standing in front of the Sheriff's station speaking to the gathering crowd of fresh recruits.

"It shouldn't take us too long to find Ruthie Joan; most of you know her, the little crippled girl who wears the leg braces," Deputy Blake said.

"Oh, yes. She couldn't have gone very far," Sam Peterson said.

"Sam, you closing up the barber shop?" Sheriff Brown asked.

"Yep. I only had Homer Jones at 10, and he's out with the Anderson crowd searchin' by the river. I'm coming with ya. Just 'cuz I'm not as young as you folks don't mean I'm not coming. Only a dirty coward would abduct a crippled child." He pulled a dark brown straw hat over his sparse grey hair and pulled out a battered Dunhill pipe.

The Secret of St. Gabriel's Tower

"When we find 'em, we should hang 'em," Buddy Shaw said, tying his horse to the hitching post next to the Sheriff's sedan.

"Now, now. I won't stand for any talk like that. If..., and I stress if, Ruthie Joan's been kidnapped, the law, and that means me and Deputy Blake, will take care of him. We have to think that she might, and I stress *might,* be a runaway."

"Runaway? She rarely went any place but school and home. Teddy came to town more than Ruthie Joan," someone in the crowd said.

"She'd need help if she was runnin' away. She doesn't even have a beau," one of women said.

"Darice's right. Ruthie Joan'd never run away. She's such a sweet child. Too trusting."

"Yep, too trusting."

"Did anyone look near Holland's Reef? The tide's been pretty rough lately."

"Holland's Reef! she couldn't get anywhere near there, not with them braces."

"What's going on?" Amber asked, as she walked pass the men who were standing in the street, near their horses or trucks. Everyone was anxious to go look for Ruthie Joan.

"Ruthie Joan's gone missing," Sam replied, tipping his hat.

"Ruthie Joan? Where could she go? She hardly goes anywhere but school and home to help her mother with the little kids. What do you mean missing?"

"Amber, I think you better ask your father for any further information," Sheriff Brown said, steering her away from the citizens and up the street a few doors to the mayor's office.

"Okay, some of you men go over to Holland's Reef and see if she might have fallen in one of the cliff fissures," Deputy Blake said, as he led a red gelding from the pasture in back of the Sheriff's office.

Amber looked back toward the dispersing crowd before entering her father's office. I just gotta get us girls back into our parent's good graces. Her eyes sparkled as the wheels in her head spun. We'll find Ruthie Joan. After all, where could she go? She's not athletic, after the polio. Actually, she wasn't athletic before the polio. She can barely walk a country mile. Uh, somebody musta kidnapped her. She leaned against the wall outside her father's door.

Knocking softly on the large mahogany door with the word, MAYOR, printed in gold letters, Amber opened it to find the somber, dark pretty face of Miss Salley Jo Smith, her father's secretary, legal assistant, old friend and her god-mother. Miss Smith, a thirty-six year old spinster, courted, for the past three years, by the local undertaker, Paul Barton. She had worked for Lincoln Walker's law firm since arriving in Poplar Cove twelve years earlier. She continued the office duties for the past two years since Linc's election. She was inserting a sheet of paper in her new Royal typewriter.

"Good Morning, Miss Salley Jo, is Daddy free?"

"Your father told me about your troubles, Amber. You continue to amaze me," Miss Smith said, slowly shaking her head.

"I'm sorry. Are you mad at me too? Mother and daddy didn't hardly speak to me this morning."

"No, I'm not angry. You're the only god-daughter I have. I don't want to have to come to your funeral 'cuz you fell off some building and got yourself killed." Salley Jo turned her back so Amber couldn't see her tears. After a few minutes she got up from her massive oak desk and walked around it and hugged Amber tighter than she ever had.

"I just didn't realize that it would be dangerous," Amber answered, returning her hug.

"Honestly, Amber! Go see your father." Salley Jo looked over at Amber, smiled for the first time that morning and continued to insert the paper in the typewriter.

♠

"Morning, Daddy."

The Secret of St. Gabriel's Tower

"Morning Amber," Lincoln said, looking up from a stack of lined yellow legal size papers. I can't remain angry at her for long, he thought. But she's going to be the death of me. She's already giving me more grey hair than my father had when he died at seventy. He pushed the papers aside lit a Lucky Strike, and waited as Amber, standing just inside the door, fiddled with the leaves of a potted palm tree.

"Mother said I had to spend the day filing."

"Filing?"

"Uh huh? she said."

"*She?*"

"Mother. Mother said that I couldn't go to school today 'cuz, ... because Robyn and Jessica would be there. They shouldn't be punished. Daddy! I talked 'em into it. I thought it would be fun. I didn't think anyone could get hurt. I never heard that any of the TriCove High boys ever got hurt," Amber sobbed. She was suddenly the little eleven-year old girl she'd been last week.

"Amber, Amber, Amber. When are you going to learn that you can't go around doing things that almost grown men do?"

"But you always said I could do anything within the law. Being a girl didn't make any difference," she thought, repeating in her mind the words her father'd told her many times. She said, "I know Daddy, I won't do it ever again."

"I know you won't. You know your mother worries, as do I. What are you going to do next?" He asked, smiling for the first time since the Sheriff arrived at his door the previous night.

"Just some filing. I can't get in trouble in the Mayor's office, now, can I?"

"No, I guess you can't. Go back and see Salley Jo, I'm sure she has plenty of things for you to file."

She turned to leave and bumped Sheriff Brown as he started to knock.

"Sorry, Amber," he said, tipping his hat." Mayor, we need more men. Can you and Homer join us?"

"Still haven't found Ruthie Joan?"

"No, sir. I don't want to believe that she's been kidnapped, but she's not in town. And she couldn't have gotten very far if she'd run away. We have to go looking in the forest. I'm having some of the older men re-search the town, again. Poplar Cove's so small, someone'd seen her if she were still here."

"I'll drive over to get Homer. Where should we meet you?"

"Deputy Blake's taking a posse up Greater Holland Road. We'll go over the Old Mill Road, meet you by the Shaw place in fifteen minutes."

"Amber, you can go home at 4:00 if I'm not back by then." Lincoln kissed the top of her forehead before following the Sheriff out the door.

"Where shall I begin?" Amber asked, walking over to Salley Jo.

"You can begin by forgetting about doing anything to find Ruthie Joan."

"I didn't say anything about trying to find her. How could I find her all by myself? The Sheriff and Deputy and a posse of men can't find her."

"They're *not* little girls. And I know you. You and the other Triplets will be in Ruthie Joan's business before sundown."

"No we won't."

♠

"Morning, Mrs. Johnson. Beautiful day isn't it?" Sam Peterson asked, tipping his hat and walking past Ruby Sue as she swept the front of her salon.

"Yes, beautiful. Terrible thing about Ruthie Joan. Who'd you think took her?" Ruby Sue replied, shading her grey eyes with her hand.

"I don't know. There were a few strangers in town yestaday, but I thought they left on the Limited," Sam said, his ever present pipe gripped tightly between his strong slightly stained teeth.

Jessica her face red streaked and dirty carried a dirty water pail and several torn rags between the small space between the buildings housing her mother's beauty salon and the Pioneer Baptist Church.

"Good morning, Mr. Peterson."

"Oh, good morning, Miss Johnson. I thought you'd be in school today."

"She's helping me," Ruby Sue added quickly.

"Oh, worried about who ever took Ruthie Joan, eh?"

"Someone took Ruthie Joan?" Putting the pail and rags on the step near her mother, Jessica looked from her mother's worried face to that of Sam Peterson.

"Jessica, take that dirty water and pour it on the rocks out back. And hang them rags on the line to dry. They're too dirty to wash. We'll burn 'em after they're dry."

"*Yesth*, Mom. 'Bye, Mr. Peterson."

"Nice girl you've got there, Mrs. Johnson."

"Most of the time. I made a pot of sun tea earlier this morning. Want some before you go looking for Ruthie Joan?"

"Some other time. I better find the posse." Tipping his hat again, he continued down Main Street.

"*Pssth. Pssth.* Mr. Peterson, over here. It's me, Jessica." Gesturing for him to come closer to her, Jessica leaned against the side of the Growers and Merchant Bank building out of sight of her mother.

"What can I do for you, Miss Johnson?"

"Tell me about Ruthie Joan."

"I... I think your mother..."

"Mom won't tell me anything. She thinks I'm a little kid. She's still mad about last night."

"Last night?"

"Uh huh, me, Amber and Robyn climbed to the top of Main Square Water tower and were writing our names..."

"Um... writing your names?"

"Uh huh, and the Sheriff told our folks. Mom and Daddy are still upset."

"I see."

"Tell me about Ruthie Joan."

"I don't know much. Her ma ain't seen her in a coupla days."

"Coupla days? She's been gone that long?"

"No, just over night. Seems Mary's been over in Marshall looking after Mrs. Young. The Sheriff has a posse or two looking for Ruthie Joan."

"Thanks. I hope you find her soon. She couldn't go far, not with her leg brace." I bet, if The Triplets could find Ruthie Joan, our parents would forget all about us climbing the tower and we could play together all summer, Jessica thought, running back to the clothes line behind her mother's shop, to hang the torn, blackened rags up to dry.

♠

Inside the Growers and Merchants Bank early Friday morning, bank president, Issac Washington, a medium height darkly tanned man with a tight smile, lit a hand rolled Cuban cigar and offered one to the only other person in the bank. "It's a little too early for brandy, but if..."

"No, I agree it's a little too early," the other man Lewis, replied. He was as expensively, if more formally, dressed. He bit the tip off the cigar and spit the end into the crystal ashtray in front of him. Smiling a gaped tooth smile and running his thin light brown right index finger over his reddish brown pencil thin moustache he said, "We have to get down to business. When will your employees arrive?" Not waiting for an answer, he reached down to the brown leather briefcase resting on the oriental rug beneath his two-tone grey and white loafer clad feet. He put it on Issac's large burl wood desk.

The Secret of St. Gabriel's Tower

"There's only three. They'll be coming in..." Taking his pocket watch out of his dark brown linen vest and looking at the Regulatory wall clock on the far wall. Issac wound the stem of his watch and continued, "in an hour. We don't open 'til 10 a.m., but most of 'em are here by 9."

"An hour. Good. We should be finished by then. What's all the activity outside? Looks like every man and boy in town was out when I got off the train this morning. I thought you said this was a quiet town."

"It is. One of the kid's is missing. A crippled girl. I'll join the search party after we've finished." Settling back in his dark green leather chair, he spoke to Lewis for nearly an hour until a 5' 10", well built, dark skinned middle aged man, knocked on the closed door. Lewis quickly closed the briefcase filled with stock certificates, a bag of gems and several small stacks of bills. Lewis settled back into the chair and twisted the diamond ring on his pinky finger and waited as he and Issac turned toward the door.

"Mr. Washington. I thought you might be out with the ... I thought you might be out. Do you or your guest need anything?"

"It's okay, Thomas."

"I don't mean to interrupt. I was just checkin' to make sure everything was okay. Mr. Washington, did you hear about little Ruthie Joan Freeman?"

"Yes, I was just getting ready to go help in the search."

"I'll be opening up in a few minutes." He nodded toward Lewis.

"Do you think he suspects anything?" Lewis asked, as soon as the door closed behind Thomas.

"No. Why should he? As far as he knows, you're just a business acquaintance. I have lots of business friends who drop by the bank early."

"Then, we're finished here. I'll be leaving for Eureka on the one o'clock train."

"You are coming back for the Juneteenth celebration at the Anderson ranch aren't you?"

"Juneteenth? I never heard of it. What's Juneteenth?"

"It's a Texas celebration about when the slaves there finally heard that they were free. We started celebrating Juneteenth about three years ago. It's almost as big as the Fourth of July in these parts, now.

About seventeen years ago, a Texas family, the Andersons, brought a large spread out east about ten miles from town. John Anderson used to go to Texas every summer for family reunions until his father died. He and the missus decided that they'd host the family reunion here in Poplar Cove and invite the town's people over for the last day. He's really into keeping the spirit alive. Invites all the folks from the Coves. Usually 400 to 500 can make it. It might be a good place to discuss our business. John's the richest man, white or colored, in these parts. He usually has a few important men from Eureka, Weed and as far away as Sacramento up for the celebration."

"I don't know. I may not be back this way til this time next year. I have to go to New York, then I'm taking the *Rotterdam* to Europe. I leave from New York in July. I'll be there for six months. There's some folks I have to see in Amsterdam. Speaking of Amsterdam, I sent you a package a few weeks ago. It should arrive today or tomorrow. Keep it in your home safe. I don't want anyone at the bank finding it by mistake."

"You can count on me. You might try to come by for the party. John Anderson might prove useful to our interest."

"So you keep telling me. Still, I don't know if it's a good idea for folks to get used to seeing me until the deal is complete. We don't want to start tongues waggin' if we don't have to."

"What we're doing is pretty risky, but we could make..." looking around and whispering Issac continued an octave lower, "millions."

"I'll call you from Eureka." Lewis reached over and shook Issac's hand.

"I'll call you no later than June 17th."

"June 17th. I'll wait for your call, Issac said, laughing. "A lot of the bank's money and my reputation are riding with you. Have a safe trip."

Lewis, laughing also, walked outside with Issac where they parted company in front of the bank. Lewis walked toward the train station but drew little attention from the few children playing in the street.

Issac returned to the bank. He picked up his Panama hat, rubbed his Justin cowboy boots on his linen trousers, and walked to his Dusenberg. He drove to the Lost Whale Tavern where he took the last fresh horse and joined the last posse.

♠

"Robyn, how are you feeling?" Ethelene asked, looking up as Robyn entered the kitchen through the back door.

"Fine."

"Whatcha doing home from school so early?"

"The sixth grade only had the history test. Mrs. Blake let us go once we finished the test. She's going over to Mrs. Johnson's to get her hair done and give the test to Jessica."

"Give the test to Jessica? Wasn't she in school today?"

"No. Mrs. Johnson and Mrs. Walker kept her and Amber home because of the water tower." She studied the tin cup on the oilcloth tablecloth like she'd never seen it before.

"The other mothers kept the girls home?"

"Yes. Mama, did you hear that Ruthie Joan is missing?"

"Missing?" Junior asked, walking into the kitchen followed immediately by Adam, each eating an oatmeal raisin cookie.

"We'll talk about it later. Take the boys outside. Walk them over to the station, they might like to see the new Limited coming in from Oregon. It should be here in an hour. Then all three of you come home with your father."

"Daddy? We're going to see daddy?" Junior asked, jumping up and down excitedly.

"You'd think he hadn't seen daddy at breakfast from the way he's acting."

"He'd spend all his time with Homer if I'd let him."

Turning toward her brother, Robyn said. "Yes, we're going to see daddy. Get your sweaters in case the fog rolls in, and I'll take you to see the new train." Leaning down she kissed the top of Junior's curly dark head before he and Adam ran from the kitchen searching for their sweaters.

"Mom, what happened to Ruthie Joan?"

"I don't know dear. Your father helped with the first posse this morning. He couldn't stay out too long because of the early mail train. He said that someone kidnapped her. That's all I know."

"Come on boys," Robyn yelled. The boys, each with a sweater on one arm, ran through the kitchen and down the steps. I bet we'd know where to look for Ruthie Joan. I have to find the others. Maybe we can go right after lunch. Robyn thought, taking Junior's hand. Adam holding on to the back step banister took the steps slowly refusing to take his sister's hand as he descended. They left the gated yard and began walking toward the train station.

♠

The Triplets, each in their own way, said, "I won't do anything to hurt myself or to bring shame to my family. Could I please, please go play with the others?"

"Have you finished the chores I gave you?"

"Yes," the Triplets replied, attempting to determine whether they were forgiven.

"I'll think about it," parents said and returned to whatever work they were doing when interrupted by their persistent daughters. By two p.m., the parents agreed to let the girls play together.

♠

41

The Secret of St. Gabriel's Tower

"Did you hear about Ruthie Joan?" Amber, the last to receive permission to meet her friends, asked as soon as the others met her in front of her father's office. They walked to the main square and sat on the park bench under the Main Square water tower.

"*Yesth,* look around," Jessica said, as she pointing up Main Street toward the train station and then beyond it to the railroad tracks that led into the forest and mountains.

"The Pacific Coast Range separates Poplar Cove from everything else in the valley. We couldn't travel over the mountains by ourselves," Amber said.

"Ruthie Joan's afraid of the ocean. She can't swim, so she'd never go near the cliffs by herself. If she went on her own she went into the forest," Robyn said.

"That means that whoever took Ruthie Joan had to have a car," Amber interrupted.

"We'll just have to check out all the cars in town, which shouldn't be hard. We can start at Mrs. Wilson's boarding house. Do we know if she has new boarders?"

"No. I did see a Stutz parked in front of her place yesterday, and Ruthie Joan disappeared sometime yesterday or early last night, didn't she?" Robyn asked.

"*Yesth,* I think so. But no one knew until real early this morning."

"I can't imagine being kidnapped and being away from my family. She must be very scared," Amber said.

"And she can't run, not with those braces. Poor thing. I wish we'd been nicer to her," Robyn stated.

"We were nice. It's just that, well, she's sort of old."

"Uh huh, she's sixteen. I saw her kissing Bobby Joe Allen, once." Amber said.

"Bobby Joe? Gee, I think he's the cutest boy in Poplar Cove. He's much younger than she is." Robyn replied.

"He's twelve. He's okay, but Three's cuter," Amber said.

"Three, he's nearly as quiet as his great grandfather. Mr. Eli Shaw hardly says anything to anyone but Miss Anna. And Three's getting more like him every day," Robyn said.

"Are we going to find out who took Ruthie Joan, or are we going to sit here talking about boys?" Jessica asked, dragging the "s" in boys out for a full second.

"We'll find Ruthie Joan. We'll check out who had the stutz and who has visitors. Most of the strangers in town are staying with families getting ready for the Juneteenth celebration. We'll began our search right after your birthday party, Robyn." Amber said.

"*Yesth,* you haven't mentioned your birthday party all morning," Jessica teased.

"You said I talk about it all the time. I decided to wait," Robyn replied.

They walked down Hill Street over to Calhoun Street towards Mrs. Wilson's boarding house, talking about who could or would kidnap Ruthie Joan. They arrived at Mrs. Wilson's in less than ten minutes.

"Hello, Mrs. Wilson," Robyn called, walking past the rose hedge in front of the pastel tricolored three story house to the rear where Mrs. Wilson knelt pulling weeds.

"Girls, how nice to see you. I see you've got some sense lately," she said, smiling and wiping damp soil particles onto her long printed cotton apron. Rushing over, Jessica and Amber helped her to her feet.

"My goodness. Thank you, but I'm not as old as you girls think. What brings you here? I'd thought that you'd be in the middle of the Sheriff's business searching for Ruthie Joan. She does go to school with you doesn't she?"

"Uh huh. We weren't at school today. Well, Robyn's Mom let her go; but Amber's Mom and mine kept us home."

"Kept you home. I heard about you girls climbing the Main water tower. You know..." bending close to the girls and whispering, although the four of them were the only ones in the yard, Mrs. Wilson said, "I always wanted to climb that tower. I

43

wanted to see how far out over the ocean I could see. So, how far could you see?"

"Not far, it was dark; and the Sheriff found us before we could do anything," Amber said regret shaping her words.

"So, are you going to tell me why you're here?" Mrs. Wilson asked, as she bent over and picked up a shallow basket of cut wild flowers and a few English roses.

"Here, let me take those. Do you have a vase to put them in?" Amber asked, taking the bouquet and walking toward the rear steps.

"Use the crystal one on the piano," Mrs. Wilson said as she and the others followed Amber up the four steps to her kitchen. The aroma of baking bread filled the large clean kitchen.

"Whatcha bakin'?" Robyn asked, her mouth watering slightly.

"Just bread for supper," Mrs. Wilson said. She pumped water over her mud browned hands and dried them on a towel next to the sink and replied, "Just bread for supper. Got a house full today. Six young women from the ranches around here. Most are going home for the summer right after the Anderson's party. Thought they were safe here in Poplar Cove, but not after the word got out about Ruthie Joan. I was up early trying to comfort them after I returned home from stayin' with Mary Freeman. Poor dears are scared to death that they'll never see their folks again. And Mary is scared to death she won't see Ruthie Joan alive," Mrs. Wilson shook her head and sucked her teeth.

"What do these women got to be scared of? They're grown. Nobody's going to kidnap a grown woman. It's not the same with Ruthie Joan. She can hardly walk," Robyn asked.

Mrs. Wilson placed a plate of warm bread in front of the girls.

"Help yourself. I made plenty."

Frowning at Mrs. Wilson's earlier words, Jessica broke off a tiny piece of hot bread and popped into her mouth.

"Well, dear, sometimes grown women need to be careful." Mrs. Wilson walked to the icebox next to the door separating the kitchen from the dining room and took out a pitcher of ice tea she took down three glasses from the cupboard above her head.

"Jessica, dear, take this icepick and chop up some ice for the tea."

"*Yesth,* ma'am."

"Iced tea, girls?"

"Yes, please." Robyn and Jessica answered.

"How's this?" Amber asked, returning to the kitchen with the flowers carefully arranged in a large tulip shaped crystal vase.

"Oh dear, they're beautiful! You have a wonderful eye for arranging. Speaking of arranging, why have you girls arranged to come see me?"

"We don't need a reason," Amber said.

"No, you don't; but you don't come together unless you're up to something. Who's going to talk first?"

"We... we... uh... we're checking out cars. In case one of your boarders took Ruthie Joan." Robyn said, softly.

"One of *my* boarders?" Mrs. Wilson replied, in mock horror.

"Uh huh, most folks, except for the regular day workers and governesses, only stay a day or so. We thought maybe someone might of seemed real nice but was really a dastardly villain," Jessica tried out her best villain voice an twirled and imaginary mustache.

"Well, I'm sorry to inform you that only the most respectable young ladies have been staying in my home for the past two weeks. None of them have probably ever seen Ruthie Joan."

"What about the person in the Stutz?" Amber asked, licking the last of the tea from her top lip.

"Stutz? Oh that was Mrs. Cora Preston, Caroline Anderson's sister. She just came by to bring me some peaches for the Juneteenth celebration. I'm making my famous peach cobbler. The Anderson's are going all out this year, and I wanted to make something everyone'd remember."

45

The Secret of St. Gabriel's Tower

"Gee, was Mrs. Preston the only boarder with a car?" Robyn asked.

"I'm afraid so dear. As all of you know, most folks walk here from the station. There really isn't a need for a car. The folks who do drive head for the Ocean View hotel in Grant's Cove."

"I guess we'll hafta look someplace else. Thanks for the tea," Amber said.

"Yes, thanks for the tea," the others mimicked in unison.

"It's always a pleasure to see you girls. Come back when you want to see me and not just look for kidnappers." Mrs. Wilson smiled and hugged each girl.

"Well that was a waste of valuable time." Jessica picked up a Shasta daisy and put it in one of her tight braids.

"We *are* going to our regular place right, St. Gabriel's Tower, for my birthday aren't we?" Robyn asked.

"Of course. It's our secret place. Our parents would never think that we'd go there," Amber replied.

"The whole town's 'fraid to go into the old mine. We're not, though."

"Are we not going to look for the car?" Amber asked.

"We'll keep a look out just in case."

"Do you think the entrance is okay?" Robyn asked, after a few minutes of silence.

"Of course, you're such a fraidy cat at times. Didn't I find the side entrance after the front got too unstable for us to play in?" Amber said.

"Besides, it's tradition for us to make our first birthday wish in the mine. We just havta go, 'specially since we were in Eureka for *my* birthday in April."

Putting their arms around Jessica, Robyn and Amber said, "but we had an extra piece of cake and ice cream to make up for celebrating late."

"Yes, we had extra cake. 'Member how my face broke out, and Mama couldn't figure out why since she'd only made one small cake?"

"I remember. It's just that the first wish really should be in St. Gabriel's."

"We better get inside. You're beginning to get all red. Your mother's already mad at the rest of us. She'll be really mad if you get sunstroke," Amber said, walking closer to the trees lining Calhoun.

"*Oogha. Oogha.*" Looking up, the Triplets waved to Reverend Fuller driving past in them in his 1927 Auburn.

"I think we can eliminate the Reverend. Somebody'd surely seen Ruthie Joan if she'd been in his fancy car," Amber said.

"Shame on you, that's your pastor!" Jessica covered her mouth in mock horror.

"Well, we have to look at *all* the cars," Amber continued.

"What ya thinkin' Robyn?" Jessica asked, as the girls walked hand in hand and crossed Carver Street to the Jefferson ice cream parlor.

"I have a secret."

"What is it?" Amber asked.

"I'll tell you in St. Gabriel's Tower," Robyn replied, thoughtfully. Maybe I should have told them that I'm a woman just like they are. I want it to be a surprise for St. Gabriel's, she thought, hugging herself.

"Still thinking?"

"Uh huh."

"Think the mice have eaten all the candles we left last October at my birthday celebration?" Amber asked.

"Maybe."

"I'll bring two from home," she continued.

"Amber, look. Isn't that Ned Simon in the back of the Sheriff's car?" Jessica ran ahead of the others and pointed to the big black Ford rushing past them heading toward the Sheriff's office.

"My gosh, Jessica, look. Is that your family's handyman, Ned, in the back seat of the Sheriff's car?" Robyn asked as the girls, along with others walking along Main Street, stared at the back of the disappearing police vehicle.

The Secret of St. Gabriel's Tower

CHAPTER

4

The Triplets walked around the rear of the Sheriff's office in an attempt to find out what was going on without attracting any more attention.

"Can you see anything?" Amber asked Robyn, who was standing on her tiptoes attempting to see the cells inside the jail.

"No. You two stay here. I'll go round front, maybe I can sneak inside without Deputy Blake seeing me."

"Why should we stay here? Why can't we go with you?" Jessica complained.

"'Cuz someone has to keep a lookout for Deputy Blake. I couldn't see if Sheriff Brown or Deputy Blake took Ned inside. It has to be me, my daddy was in the first posse." The girls with their backs pressed against the rear of the Sheriff's Office looked around the field, searching for any grown ups who might stop them. The Sheriff's gelding and a few circling butterflies were in the field. The horse whinnied a greeting and went back to eating hay near the far fence.

The Secret of St. Gabriel's Tower

"I'll be back in a few minutes if I can't get in. If I can, I'll open the back door; and we'll interview Ned." Without waiting for her friends' reply, Robyn walked quickly around the side of the building and bumped into Sheriff Brown on the sidewalk in front of the jail.

"Hello, Robyn."

"Hello, Sheriff. I... we saw Ned Simon in the back of your car a little while ago. What's he done?"

"You'd better go home. Deputy Blake and I have work to do. I don't think your parents want me bringing you home twice in one week."

"Oh, I was just wondering."

"Good bye, Robyn. Tell the others to go home also." Sheriff Brown waited until Robyn retraced her steps and disappeared. Smiling to himself he opened the door and patted his shirt pocket.

"Need cigars," he said to himself and started to cross the street to the Jefferson Five and Ten Cents Store and Ice Cream Parlor.

♠

"Psst... girls, follow me," Robyn gestured to the others to follow her as she walked quickly toward the meadow behind the jail, scratching a fresh pimple.

"Did you find out anything?" Amber asked.

"Do they think that Ned has anything to do with Ruthie Joan?"

"I couldn't find out anything. The Sheriff said that he might have to escort me home. I wouldn't get out at all this summer if he brought me home again. I couldn't see if Ned was locked up."

"Gosh, I guess we'll have to find out about what's going on some other way," Amber said, splashing warm water from a horse trough in front of Buddy Shaw's blacksmith shop on her sweating face. Then she took a hand full of water and splashed both of her friends. The girls, giggling and shaking water off their hands at each other walked toward Hill Street.

♠

"Ain't you the youngest of the Simons boys from up in Marshall Cove?" Deputy Blake asked.

"Yes, Sir. Why'd you pick me up? I ain't done nothin'."

"Answer my questions first. How long ya been livin' in Poplar Cove?"

"'Bout six...no seven years. What's this all about? I said I ain't done nothin'."

"The Sheriff's bringin' the evidence with him."

"What evidence? What've I've suppose to have done?"

"Sheriff will answer your questions. He'll be here in a few minutes. Come with me to this cell. He'll talk to you there."

Deputy Blake sat down on a chair outside the cell with a lined writing pad on his knee.

"What about my book? I left my book over off Adams Street where I was choppin' wood for the Johnson's. Come on Edwain, you know me. Tell me how long ya gonna keep me locked up?"

"I'll have someone pick up your book for you. What's it called?"

"*Darkwater* by Mr. W. E. B. du Bois. Homer Jones lent it to me. It's pretty good. Hard to understand. You ever read it?"

"No. I haven't. You aren't distracting me from what I have to do. Sit down, relax. I have some questions to ask. I need to fill in some information Sheriff Brown will need for his report. How old are you?"

"Twenty-five this past May."

"Weight? About 230, I'd say."

The Secret of St. Gabriel's Tower

"Closer to 250. The entire family is big boned." Ned replied, shyly he looked through the cell bars, his large light brown hands gripping the bars tightly. Wetting the end of his pencil, Deputy Blake looked over at the young man ten years his junior. I can't believe this man kidnapped that girl. He could be my younger brother Kenneth's twin. Look at him, the same nondescript color of dried leaves, the same smile as Kenny. There, but for the Grace of God, could be Kenny. I have to write Ma and find out what Kenny's doing, Edwain Blake thought, licking the pencil again.

"Ned, I..."

"Edwain? You in the back?"

"In here, Sheriff. I was just gettin' the vitals on Ned."

"Did he say where Ruthie Joan is?" The Sheriff asked.

"Who's Ruthie Joan?" Ned asked.

"The little crippled girl that you took."

"Took? I haven't took, uh, taken anyone. What do you mean took?" Ned replied, jumping up from the narrow cot and reaching through the bars toward the Sheriff.

"Ruthie Joan is missing," Sheriff Brown said, stepping away from the bars.

"Missing? Why'd you think I'd know anything about her?"

"Her hair ribbon."

"What hair ribbon?" Ned asked, still reaching through the bars.

"Sit down, Ned. Sit down!" Sitting down and dragging the cot closer to the bars, Ned waited for the Sheriff to continue.

"The girl's hair ribbon was found in your room. Right under the window in a corner. You don't keep a very tidy home, but we found it right with the nut husks, shells, twigs and other things you keep safe, like," Sheriff Brown replied, unwrapping a cigar and biting off the end. Walking around Deputy Blake and pulling up a chair he sat down. The chair creaked under his weight.

"I ain't never had a girl at my place. No one there but me and Wally," Ned interrupted.

"Wally?" Deputy Blake asked.

"My pet raccoon."

"We're not talking about raccoons. We're talking about ribbons like this one," Sheriff Brown continued, ignoring Ned and Deputy Blake's interruptions. Taking a narrow pale green ribbon from his left breast pocket, Sheriff Brown said, "This was found under the window next to your bed. Now tell me where'd you hide the girl? She is still alive isn't she?"

"Of course, she's still alive," Ned shouted, his voice catching on the last word, a strangled 'alive'.

"Sheriff, Edwain, you both know me. I stay by myself. I'm not too familiar round folks. I seen the little crippled girl, but I never said nothing to her or her Ma. I wouldn't hurt her. I didn't even know her name. Only a monster would hurt a cripple..." Ned continued, between sobs. Sitting down heavily on the cot and covering his face with his hands, he sobbed loudly while the Sheriff and Deputy looked first at each other then at him.

"Edwain, let's leave him to think about what he's done." Getting up and pushing the chair against the far wall, Sheriff Brown and Deputy Blake left the still sobbing Ned alone in his cell.

"Sheriff, he seems pretty broken up. I don't think he took her. But she's still missin', and her ribbon was found in his cabin."

"Ned's never been in trouble before. Keeps to himself. Doesn't even visit Miss Alice's or The Lost Whale Tavern to hear folks talk. Still, as my grandmother's fond of saying, 'still waters runs deep'. We'll keep him locked up until we find someone else or he decides to talk. I'm not ready to admit to a mistake, not yet."

"Zachary, do you think he'll be okay in here?"

"Yes, why?"

"Ruthie Joan's brother, Teddy, got liquored up at the Lost Whale earlier today and said some things he wouldn't have if he'd been sober."

"I'll have Cal Robinson go over and talk to him. Teddy's a good kid. He won't do anything unless ..."

"Unless she's dead," Edwain Blake said, solemnly.

"I have to believe that whoever's got her has her alive. We're probably missing something right in front of our noses; and,

53

The Secret of St. Gabriel's Tower

if we don't find out what it is, those Triplets will be in the middle of our business."

"Oh, no, not the Triplets."

"Yes, Robyn ran into me as I was coming in. It was all I could do to not to have her follow me into the station. Knowin' her she'd be questioning the prisoner before we could," the Sheriff said, chewing on the still unlit cigar.

"We'll just tell their parents to keep them away from our investigation," Deputy Blake answered as he sat on the edge of the Sheriff's desk and thumbed through a stack of yellowed wanted posters.

"Edwain, you've only been in Poplar Cove for a short time. This isn't Birmingham. The Triplets do just about whatever they want. They're basically good girls, but they are very nosy. If they get involved, it won't be the first time. They've found missing jewelry, captured a burglar over at the station when they were sittin' in for Homer. Remember when we caught them dancing in the field behind Miss Ruby's Jute Joint, earlier this year? They'd been peeking at all the dandies and their ladies wondering why they couldn't go inside if all folks was doing was dancing. Remember? Their folks had them on restrictions for over a week, and *they're only eleven*!" Sheriff Brown said, rubbing his blood shot eyes.

"I'm tired. I haven't been sleeping all night. I don't like the summer. Too many strangers around. People do strange things when it gets hot. We're not used to this weather. It should be in the high sixties. It's mid June, and already we've had three days over 90 degrees. It's much too hot for the coast. Now this, with Ruthie Joan." Getting up from his chair and tossing his hat onto the crowded hat rack in the corner of his office, Sheriff Brown loosened his tie and walked toward the back door.

"I need some fresh air. I need to think. Could you go over to Henrietta's and bring back some lunch for Ned and me? Get some for yourself. I think it's going to be a long day."

"Sure Zachary. Anything in particular?"

"Nope. Whatever you want get the same for Ned and me." Sheriff Brown walked outside and pumped water over his head and face, stretched his back and rubbed his eyes. He looked over the dried grassy field behind the jail toward the front of Henry's Garage and sighed. He took a carrot from the shelf just inside the jail and walked over to his horse, Red Ranger. He patted the horse's neck as he fed him the carrot and thought what is this world coming too? He thought. A kid I've known since he first came to Poplar Cove is in my jail suspected of abducting a crippled child. Giving the horse an extra pat, he reentered the jail and walked back to the cell containing Ned Simon.

♠

"Ned, Mrs. Freeman says that Hattie told her that Ruthie Joan was wearing this ribbon the last time anyone saw her. Yes, sir, wearing this very ribbon that was found in your home. Now tell me again where were you and did anyone see you?"

"I was fishing, alone. I din't see nobody. I was on the upper fork of the river. I din't do nothin' to that girl. I only seed her once or twice and only with her Ma. I never hurt nobody," Ned said, his speech reverting back to the country slang of Kentucky as if seeking comfort in the sounds of familiar words. "Sheriff, you know I din't do nothin', honest."

"The ribbon?"

"The wind musta blown it into my room. I never touched her. Never."

CHAPTER

5

"We've looked at every car, truck and wagon in Poplar Cove; none of them contain Ruthie Joan," Jessica said, wiping perspiration from her reddened face as she and the others walked up Hill street.

"We know everyone who has a car. I didn't see any strangers about who weren't with really really respectable folks," Robyn said.

"I guess we'll just have to find out what the town's folks know."

"Yes, that's what we have to do. Robyn, you go over to the train station and find out what you can about Ruthie Joan from your father. He might tell you something he hasn't told the Sheriff. He was in the first posse. He might have clues that he doesn't know he has," Amber said, walking quickly in an attempt to keep up with her two taller friends.

"I just came from there. I walked the boys over earlier. Daddy wouldn't say anything."

"Well, go look for suspicious folks then."

"Okay. I doubt if anyone mysterious is getting on any of our trains."

"We'll meet back here in an hour and compare notes. Jessica, you go to your mother's beauty shop. Someone's bound to have some idea what really happened to Ruthie Joan. Lots of folks stand in front of her and Mr. Peterson's place and talk for hours."

"Where're you going?" Robyn asked.

"I'm going to see my father. I'm going to tell him that Ned couldn't have done anything ...couldn't have done anything to Ruthie Joan."

"We know that. But grown ups aren't going to take our word that someone else kidnapped her."

Reaching the top of the hill the girls went their separate ways. Amber walked past the third posse regrouping in front of the town square. Waving to them, she burst into her father's office. He was alone studying the corps of engineers' drawings of a new dam. He looked up. His face was a study of frustration.

"Amber, can't you see that I'm busy. I didn't get any rest today looking all over for Ruthie Joan. I don't have time for you this afternoon."

"But, daddy, Ned..," she began. Then, seeing the questioning look in her father's dark eyes, she continued, "...I mean, Mr. Simons, well he couldn't 'uve done 'nothin' to Ruthie Joan. We... all us kids know that he's harmless."

"This be the work of adults, Amber Leigh. I don't have time for any of your nonsense. You're still in trouble for climbing the water tower. Your mother may've forgiven you, but I haven't. I can't believe that you wrote your name on the tank for all the world to see, shaming me. Us. I'm the mayor. You're our daughter. You need to set an example."

"But, Daddy..."

He leaned back in his wine colored leather chair. It was a sign with which she was very familiar. Her father was finished talking. He folded his hands across his flat stomach and waited for her to leave. Standing next to him for a few minutes, Amber sighed and said,"Okay, bye, daddy." She leaned over and kissed the top of his balding head. If he won't listen, then Robyn, Jessica and I will just have to find Ruthie Joan on our own, she thought. She closed the door and walked outside just as Salley Jo returned from an errand.

"Can I help you, Amber?"

"No, thanks, Miss Salley Jo. I've seen daddy."

"Well goodbye, dear. You going home?"

"No," Amber replied, in a barely audible voice. "I was ganna...I mean. I was going to spend the day with Robyn and Jessica. Today's Robyn's birthday celebration."

"My my, tell her happy birthday for me."

"Thank you." Amber ran across Main street to the far side of the town square. She didn't see her father standing in front of his window watching her.

"I wonder how long it's going to take for her to get into trouble."

"Are you speaking to me, Mr. Mayor?" Salley Jo asked, putting a roll of plans on his desk.

"No, Salley Jo. I was talking to myself. Amber just left; and I know, deep in my bones, that she and the others are not going to let the Sheriff look for Ruthie Joan unassisted. She's going to be the death of me. I'm too old for this."

"Old? Why, Mr. Mayor, you're just a youngster."

"Amber's aged me. I'm a lot older than 36," he replied, smiling. "I can't remain angry at her. Mable and I always wanted an independent child. Little did we realize that our wish would come true tenfold. Let's get to work on these plans if I'm going to be ready for the city council tomorrow."

♠

"Did you find out anything?" Amber asked as she sat down next to Robyn at the Jefferson's Five and Ten Cents Store and Ice

The Secret of St. Gabriel's Tower

Cream Parlor. She looked around. They were the only fountain customers. Two women came in and purchased bolts of calico and left.

"Not really. There was a nice looking colored man waiting for the local. He was dressed like Mr. Washington at the bank usually does. He was wearing a tan pin striped suit and some really fancy shoes. He bought a copy of the Eureka Times. Daddy said he missed yesterday's Eureka train. He was real mad. But he walked back to town, musta stayed with someone. I think he must be a banker from up north. He didn't notice me at all," Robyn replied.

"I didn't find out anything. My father's still angry. I better stay out of mother's way," Amber said.

"Daddy said that one of Ruthie Joan's ribbons was found in Ned's bedroom. Daddy was with the search team. They went by Ned's place to ask him to join them. He wasn't at home. He never locks his doors. I don't think anyone does. One of the men saw a ribbon lying on the floor near Ned's bed. Everyone know's that Ned doesn't have a girl," Jessica, in her most theatrical voice, slowly emphasized each word.

"Are you sure that's what your dad said?" Amber asked. "Mine won't say anything to me about Ruthie Joan. I bet you're just making this up. You've been play acting ever since we went to the moving picture house in Grant's Cove six months ago. You haven't been the same since."

"I told you that you could write for me. I'll be a famous actress in the moving pictures. Mom said it didn't matter that I lisp 'cuz no one would know, seeing as moving pictures are silent."

"Did you see any colored folks that we know in the moving pictures? We all can't be Ethel Waters. Besides, she lives in New York or somewhere back east where all the moving pictures are made. Am I right? Well, am I?" Amber countered.

Jessica didn't say anything. "Well, did you see anyone you knew? No. You're gonna stay in Poplar Cove and marry some boy from Grant's Cove and have a bunch of kids. While I'll write and go to Paris," Amber teased.

"Neither of you are going anywhere but Poplar Cove. We'll all marry boys from Marshall or Grant's Cove," Robyn said."Or... or maybe three not so mysterious strangers'll git off the train and marry us," she continued.

"You're always dreaming of someone coming to Poplar Cove on the train."

"I want to hear 'bout the ribbon," Amber interrupted.

"That's all I know. I overheard daddy talking to Mr. Peterson. They stopped talking when I came closer, like I was a little kid or something."

"Amber, Jessica, ya know Ned couldn't do anything to hurt Ruthie Joan. He's ... well, shy. 'Member how he'd stammer whenever he'd try talking to us? He wouldn't hurt a fly," Robyn said, absently rubbing a fresh pimple. She crossed herself and continued. "What if we're wrong? What if Ned had someone hurt Ruthie Joan? We've never experienced anything remotely exciting like a disappearance of somebody we know."

"Books'll tell ya most folks don't really know each other. We all got our dark side," Amber said, attempting to regain control of her mystery.

"You Triplets gonna sit here all morning, or are ya gonna order somethin'?" Hiram Jefferson asked. He peered over his glasses. He stood next to their booth, his arms resting on his ample stomach.

"I'll have a vanilla shake," Robyn said.

"Strawberry."

"Do you have any chocolate?" Amber asked.

"Yes, we have chocolate. One of these days you girls are going to order something beside your usual and I'll know that you're imposters." Giggling, the Triplets smiled as Mr. Jefferson walked away with their predictable orders.

"Who's that with Mr. Thomas?" Robyn asked, pointing to two figures coming from the Growers and Merchants' Bank. Hiram Jefferson placed the three milk shakes in front of the girls and walked away. They continued to look out the window.

The Secret of St. Gabriel's Tower

"Where?" Amber asked, squinting in the direction of Robyn's point. "I don't see anyone."

"You *do* need glasses. There are two men not five hundred feet in front of you. Mr. Thomas and a really nicely dressed stranger."

"I *don't* need glasses. The sun's in my eyes. Maybe the stranger took Ruthie Joan," she said.

"I doubt anyone Mr. Thomas be seen with would take anyone from Poplar Cove. I heard Mama and Dad saying that butter wouldn't melt in his mouth. Mama said that he thinks he's too good for Poplar Cove. He want's to own Mr. Washington's bank and move to San Francisco and go to the opera and ballet," Robyn continued.

"My Aunt Annabelle goes to the opera and the ballet. She's really nice. So is Uncle Philip. Nice people go to the opera," Amber said, as she sucked chocolate off the bottom of a straw.

"Mama says Mr. Thomas puts on airs," Robyn added, wiping a vanilla moustache off her top lip.

"Look, that man is getting into the front seat of Mr. Thomas' car," Jessica said.

"Well whoever he is he must be a close friend of Mr. Thomas. He's sitting right up front, not even Mrs. Thomas sits in the front seat," Robyn answered.

"I agree. I haven't seen anybody in The Cove sit in the front seat. Whoever he is, he must be very important. I wonder what they're talking about. Mr. Thomas sure looks very excited."

"Too bad you can't see him. You could ask your daddy what he's doing here," Robyn said, turning toward Amber who squinted in the direction of the fuzzy figures.

"I'm not interested in any stranger that's sitting in the middle of Main Street with the bank teller. Whoever he is, he isn't our kidnapper."

"Speaking of excitement, when are we going to go to St. Gabriel's? Do we hafta find Ruthie Joan first?" Robyn interrupted.

"No, we'll go right away," Amber replied, putting two nickels on the table next to her and Robyn's empty shake glasses.

"My treat," she said, handing Robyn a gift-wrapped in hand-dyed orange paper. "Here's the silver locket you admired in Marie's Fine Clothing's window last year," Amber said, not waiting for Robyn to unwrap the gift.

"I have something for you also." Taking a small cloisonne pin from her overall pocket, Jessica unwrapped it before handing it over to Robyn.

"You both are so special," Robyn replied, getting up and hugging each girl.

"Let's go to St. Gabriel's before it gets too hot."

Getting up, they waved good-bye to Mr. Jefferson and walked out of the store and down Main Street. They crossed the railroad tracks and walked east toward St. Gabriel's Tower.

CHAPTER 6

Amber sat down in the dirt along the side of the hard, dusty trail. She removed her left shoe and shook out a small pebble.

"Wait for me," she yelled to the others. They had continued up the meandering trail until it split joining another wider road.

"Okay," Robyn yelled back. She ran her fingers over her new locket.

Amber took off her other shoe and tied the shoestrings together. She slid one shoe through the armhole of her overalls; then, barefoot like the others, she ran to join them. She asked, "Where's the fog when you need it? It's too hot to be June. We'll die by October if this heat keeps up." She wiped sweat from her eyes and smudged the dirt on her face. She ran her short fat fingers through her damp, curly, black, dust covered hair. Her *"Shirley Temple"* ringlets fell to the middle of her back. She pulled at her sticky undershirt and licked beads of perspiration from her top lip.

"I'm hot. Walk in the shade," Amber said after a few minutes.

"How are we gonna find someone our daddies haven't been able to find?" Jessica asked as she pulled at one of her dark red braids. It had given up the struggle to remain in place in the humid air. Her left braid, not to be ignored, stuck out to the side like a railroad crossing arm. Amber looked over at her and laughed.

"What's so funny?"

"You look like a Raggedy Anne doll."

"What?"

"Raggedy Anne. Member, I saw a picture of one in your mom's shop? You're all red and freckly like those dolls. At least your mother lets you wear your hair in braids. I always have to wear these stupid ringlets. They're always in the way." Amber pulled Jessica closer to the shade. Jessica's face was beet red, and her undershirt was soaked.

"JJ, go stand under the tree. Where's your hat? You know your mama's going to be angry if you lose another one," Robyn walked over to the shade and stood by Jessica.

"I asked how are we?"

"Cuz, we're the Triplets," Amber answered. "Where would we go if we were hiding from our folks? Course, I don't know why Ruthie Joan would be hiding from her folks. I bet she's never done anything half as daring as writing her name on a water tower. She wouldn't even go with us this spring when we went over to Miss Alice's to listen to the music. 'Course she said, she wouldn't come 'cuz of her leg, but I think she's just shy. Besides, if she did, where'd she go?"

"St. Gabriel's Tower!" The other two shouted in unison.

"Right, grown-ups never think to look there. I bet it never even occurred to them that she might be there," Amber skipped toward the mountain. Robyn and Jessica were right behind her.

"But didn't they look near there last year when that little boy, what's his name... Billy, disappeared?" Robyn asked.

"Remember the scare the town had when Billy wandered away from his family's campsite?" Amber asked.

"He was only three. I remember looking for him for hours after school. Thank goodness, that we found him," Robyn added.

"And he was okay. We'll find Ruthie Joan... and uh... and uh... she'll be okay, too," Jessica said.

"Billy wasn't anywhere near St. Gabriel's. He wandered off into the forest," Amber said. "The town's folks haven't gone near St. Gabriel's in years."

"Folks don't think that *we'd* go to St. Gabriel's. Ned'd never go there. He's 'fraid of the dark."

"Oh, and how do you know that?" Robyn asked.

"I know because he works for daddy, and he won't go near the woods at night. I can't imagine him in the mine. Wait, why would Ruthie Joan go into St. Gabriel's? She's as afraid of it as the rest of the town's people. She'd never go in there. We have to think of someplace else."

"Someplace where the kidnappers would hide her." Amber added.

"I can't think of anyplace else. Maybe we can think better when we're no so hot." Fanning the hot moist air Jessica moved closer to the shade.

"*Yesth*. Maybe she's in Marshall Cove. She could be tied up in one of those abandoned houses, the Chinese folks lived in years ago."

"In the ghost town?" Amber boomed, with excitement.

"Uh huh."

"How are we going to get there?" Robyn asked over Jessica's growling stomach.

"I'm starving, too. We should have eaten something. That milk shake just made me more hungry. We'll never be able to walk to Marshall Cove. What time is it?" Amber asked.

"Nearly one." Jessica carefully opened the case of an old ornate silver pocket watch from her overalls pocket. The watch was decorated with swirls that looked like the initials, JJJ.

"I'm hungry and thirsty. Vanilla always makes me thirsty."

The Triplets continued walking toward St. Gabriel's when they heard a noise and stopped.

♠

"Shush... do you hear somethin?" Amber asked.

"I hear voices," Jessica said.

"So do I," Robyn said.

"Where's it comin' from?" Robyn pointed to a clearing about 500 yards in front of them. They ducked behind a small tree and peered into the clearing. Two men were fly fishing in the stream.

"Do we know them?" Amber asked.

"No. They're colored men, though. Probably from Grant's Cove. We know most of the people in Marshall Cove."

"I can see they're colored. I just couldn't make out their faces," Amber said, her voice startling small animals and birds.

♠

"What was that?" one man asked. They moved closer to the river's bank turned and listened to the forest sounds.

"I only hear the chirping of the birds and the sound of the stream," the second one said. He cast his line back into the swift stream.

♠

"I'm certain the men can hear our hearts pounding, Amber whispered, pulling Jessica with her on the far side of a large sequoia. "Quick let's get behind a sequoia; this little tree wouldn't hide a cat. We can stand side by side in the tree's shadow and not be seen."

"They're probably just fishermen," Robyn said. "I'll go over and ask them if they've seen Ruthie Joan."

"Are you crazy? They probably murdered Ruthie Joan and they'll murder us too if they catch us."

"We've never seen real murderers before," Robyn said. Her teeth chattered in the heat. Her body shook. She stamped her numb feet to warm them up.

"I think we're trapped. We can't get back to the road without the men seeing us," she said after a few seconds. The girls held their breath and inched around the tree. They kept the men in sight.

♠

"I don't hear anything. Are you sure that it wasn't a chipmunk or something?" the second man asked. The first man leaned his head to one side as if he were listening for something just out of range. He walked out of the stream and knelt by a small campfire.

♠

Robyn peered around the tree and described the campsite for Amber. "It's littered with fish bones, half filled tin coffee cups and two tin plates. Ugh..."

"What?" Amber croaked. She put her hand over her mouth when the men turn in her direction.

"Don't try to talk. Your voice carries in the forest."

"I..."

"Shush. I was going to say that there are still remnants of scrambled eggs and fish stuck to the tin plates. And there's an old truck. Looks like it might be a 1921 Ford hidden in the trees behind the camp. I can't see the license plate."

"We should go over to the truck and see if Ruthie Joan's tied up in there," Jessica began moving toward the truck.

"Wait, stay here. Between Amber's foghorn voice and your lisp, they're going to hear us. I'm the only one with a normal voice. What's that?" Robyn asked, as she pointed to two dull brown blankets rolled up near a rotting tree stump.

"Just blankets."

"Let's get to the other side where Amber can talk," she continued.

"Are we sure they're fishermen?" Amber asked, her voice carrying away from the men.

"I guess so. They're dressed like fishermen. Both are wearing worn levis, faded cotton plaid shirts and thick waders," Robyn said.

"Describe them for me. Maybe I've seen them in town," Amber demanded.

"Okay, one, the taller, fatter of the two, is wearing a dirty grey cap with fish lures attached to the cap's bill. They're both clean-shaven, about your coloring, you know, kind of light tan. The other is very short barely as tall as we are. He's wearing an ugly battered, dark blue, uh. What did your Uncle Philip call the hat he gave you from the ship?"

"A watch cap," Amber replied.

"Uh huh, a watch cap. The other man's wearing a watch cap."

"Is there anything on it?"

"On it? Like what?" Robyn asked.

"You said one man's hat had fish lures. Does the watch cap have lures too?"

"No."

"Do you see any guns?" Amber asked.

"No."

"Well, Jeb, I don't hear anything now," the first man said.

"When we're finished here, do you think we should look in that old mine up yonder that we passed last night?" the second man asked, pointing in the direction of St. Gabriel's Tower.

"No, town folks says no one's been there in years." A light breeze blew the men's words away from the Triplets. Hearing bits and pieces of the men's conversation, they jumped on the last clear word, *mine.*

"They've got her in the mine," Amber said, speaking over what the first man was saying. "We'll have to sneak around them and find her."

"They said that no one'd been in the mine. I don't want those men to discover us listening to their plans."

"They just said that in case someone was listening," countered Amber. "I'm goin' even if you two don't."

"We could be in *real* danger, not the little danger like climbing the water tank. Someone could get hurt," Robyn said after a few minutes. She had not moved from her spot behind the tree.

"I already said I was going." Amber stepped carefully around the tree while she kept the men in her fuzzy gaze.

"We can't let you go alone. If we don't go, you'll try to find Ruthie's body by yourself and what if the murderer found you?" Robyn stammered. She was so scared that she leaned over by the tree to throw up but the moment passed. "How could we tell your mom and dad that we let their daughter chase murderers by herself? You almost made me throw up." She hit Amber on the shoulder and began to cry.

"I'm sorry but I'm going," Amber said. She hugged Robyn.

♠

"I tell ya, Willie, there's something out there," the man wearing the grey cap said. The girls made themselves as small as possible and quietly crept around the giant tree through the underbrush, until they were out of immediate danger.

♠

"I hope the roar of this stream will hide any unusual sounds that we make," Amber said, as the girls scrambled deeper into the woods. "I can still hear the men."

"Me, too. I can't make out their words."

"At least you can talk normally without waking up the dead," Robyn said. "I didn't mean..." she continued. She put her hand over her mouth and leaned against a tree. A few minutes later the nausea in her stomach passed.

"We know you weren't talking about Ruthie Joan," Amber and Jessica said, giving her a reassuring hug.

♠

"Are we going the right way?" Jessica asked, after they'd traveled a couple of miles through the winter's accumulation of thick underbrush.

"Yes. It rained a lot this spring. Everything's gotten overgrown and wild," Robyn said. "We've had to circle back so we wouldn't be found by those men. But this is the way."

"Something's wrong. Look, the spiders' webs are broken," Amber said, pointing to the spider web free opening at the side of St. Gabriel's Tower.

"And the front of the opening is smooth, as if..."

"As if someone or something has been dragged inside," Jessica finished as she knelt down into the moist earth and ran her hands over the deep ruts that disappeared into the dark mine.

"I told you they put Ruthie Joan's body in *our* mine," Amber said, as she looked into the mine's narrow opening.

"We don't know that she's in there," Jessica said biting her trembling bottom lip.

"I'll find out. Ruthie Joan... Ruthie Joan, are you in there? It's me, Amber Walker." Amber's voice echoed back to her from the interior of the mine. Two small field mice scurried over her bare feet causing her to jump.

"Ruthie Joan, can you hear us?" she called again.

"We're here also, JJ and Robyn," the others said in barely audible voices. Waiting a few seconds the Triplets listened at the mine's opening.

"I guess we have to go in and see if she's there," Robyn said.

"*Ooh. Ooh.*"

"What is that?" the three asked, taking a giant step away from the opening.

The Secret of St. Gabriel's Tower

"Did you hear that low moan? It's too late for bears to still be hibernating. Isn't it?" Robyn asked.

Amber took two tentative steps toward the opening. "Ruthie Joan?" she called, cautiously in a small voice that even she didn't recognize.

"Ooh. Ooh."

"There's someone in there!" Amber said. She bent over put on her shoes. She ran into the mine. Jessica and Robyn followed closely behind her.

"It's me," A barely audible, hysterical voice said from deep within the mine.

"Ruthie Joan? Don't move; just keep talking. We'll get you out of there. I have a candle somewhere," Amber said, searching her overalls pockets.

"Did anyone remember to bring matches?" Robyn asked.

"I did. I always have them in case... you know... for cigarettes." Jessica took a broken match, a tobacco pouch and loose tobacco from her top left overalls pocket. "I think smokin' glamorous. All the moving picture actresses smoke," she continued, "I don't care that you two don't like it. Besides I only smoke once in a while."

She struck the match on a dry rock and lit one of Amber's candles. The girls went further into the mine. The candle's dim light outlined the rotting overhead beams and crumbling walls.

"Look. The old beam's fallen across the entrance," Robyn said. "Looks like the main pathway is blocked." All the color drained from her face as she looked at the spot on the ground.

"Bloo...blood!" She ran outside and threw up.

"Jessica, those *are* drops of blood," Amber croaked, her face drained of color. Jessica stood trembling a few inches from the blood.

"Do... do you see her?" Jessica closed her eyes tight.

"No."

"Do you see anything? I'm afraid to look." Jessica trembled as she handed the candle to Amber.

"The floor is disturbed. There are two deep lines *drawn* in the dirt."

"Drawn in the dirt?" Jessica opened her eyes and looked down at the marks highlighted by the candlelight.

"It looks like a trail. Like someone's been dragged further into the mine," Amber said. Flashes of yellow streaks from the mine walls caught the candlelight whenever the girls moved the candle.

"It's me, Ruthie Joan. I can't move. I don't think he's breathin'. I think he's dead. I just wanted to ... *AHHHH, AHHHH*" the rest of the sentence was cut off by a blood curdling scream.

"Ruthie Joan!" Amber yelled, as she leaned closer to the fallen wall.

"Please, please get us out of here," Ruthie Joan cried hysterically.

"Ruthie Joan? I'm here," Amber answered. Robyn began crying loudly. She drowned out Ruthie Joan's words.

"Are you alright? There's blood all over the floor," Amber asked, her voice shaking.

"I'm ... I'm scared. I want my mama. Where's mama? Is she with you? Mama?"

"Don't cry, Ruthie Joan. We'll get you out. Your mama has the entire town looking for you. What are you doing in the mine?"

"My brace is broken. I can't walk," Ruthie Joan sobbed.

"What do you mean, you can't walk?" Amber asked, her voice tinged with hysteria.

GROAN, CRACK, GROAN, CRASH. The beam above the girl's heads slipped. They ran outside seconds before it fell directly where they'd been standing. The Triplets sat down on the pine needles covering the ground in front of the mine's entrance. Their faces were streaked with dirt, and their hair was full of dust. Their eyes were bloodshot with fear and from crying.

"Oh please, God, don't let them die," Robyn sobbed. She crossed herself and wiped her runny nose on her shirtsleeve. Fresh pimples dotted her sweating forehead.

The Secret of St. Gabriel's Tower

"That wish don't count as your birthday wish," Jessica said. Dust still billowed from the mine's entrance.

"How are we going to get her out of there? How did she get in there? Who's she with?" Amber asked.

"We hafta get our daddies. They'll know what to do," Robyn said. She placed her right hand over her mouth. After a second her color returned.

"I'll go to town. I can run faster than you two," Amber said, not budging. "Maybe someone should find those men we saw earlier. Maybe they could get Ruthie Joan out."

Robyn and Jessica gasped.

"Well they can't be murderers if Ruthie Joan's in the mine. She didn't say she was forced into the mine now did she?" Amber asked.

"What 'bout the blood?" Robyn asked.

"Can't be Ruthie Joan's. She sounded scared out of her wits, but not hurt. Perhaps it was animal blood. Since I'm wearing shoes, I'll go and try and find the men. Perhaps they can help us move the beam and get Ruthie Joan out. You two try to find out who's in there with her and if he's hurt really bad," Amber said. She jumped up, ran off and retraced their path to where they left the men fishing.

♠

Amber reached the men's campsite in half the time it took the girls to reach the mine. Not stopping to catch her breath she boomed, "You gotta help us! Our.... friend's trapped... in the mine. She maybe hurt real bad. There's blood..." Amber leaned against a small tree gasping for breath. Her normally deep voice sounded a full octave lower. She pointed back in the direction she'd just run from. The men dropped their fishing poles in the stream as she burst into the clearing. They helped her sit down on a large rock next to the dying campfire.

"Whoever's with Ruthie Joan,... my... our friend, could be dead."

"Take it easy, miss. You're with friends. We won't let anyone hurt you. Did someone kidnap you? We heard talk last night that some girl from around here got took. You her?" Jeb asked, as he poured water into one of the tin cups. Amber's hands shook as she took it from him.

"No, no. Ruthie Joan was kidnapped. My name's... my name's Amber Walker. My father's the Mayor of Poplar Cove. My friend, Ruthie Joan, she's in the mine," Amber replied.

"I'm Jeb Dixon from Weed; this here'n my friend, Willie Boyd, from near Marshall Cove. We've come for the fishin.' Now, how can we help you, miss?"

"You said one of your friends is in the mine?" Willie asked as he walked to the truck. He searched around for a second and took out a shotgun and rifle from under the seat. He walked back to where Amber and Jeb sat and split the shotgun open. He loaded shells into it and into the rifle.

"We better be prepared if there's kidnappers about," he said as Amber stared opened mouthed at him.

"I think the kidnapper may be trapped inside St. Gabriel's with Ruthie Joan," Amber said.

"St. Gabriel's?"

"The mine back there. We hafta hurry. My other friends, Jessica and Robyn and me, we tried to move the beam that holds the ceiling. But it was heavy even though it started coming apart right in our hands." She swallowed another sip of water. Then she continued, "And we couldn't see 'cuz the candle went out, and Robyn was crying. We were all scared. More scared than I've ever been," Amber said. She handed the cup back to Jeb. He poured the last drops onto the smoldering embers.

"We thought that you might be the missing girl from the way ya burst into camp," Willie said, spitting tobacco juice inches from the dying fire.

"I was inna hurry to find you."

"To find us?"

79

The Secret of St. Gabriel's Tower

"Uh huh. We saw you earlier this afternoon, but we thought you were murderers. We hid from you and went to the mine and found Ruthie Joan."

"Oh, you thought we were murderers?" Jeb asked.

"Yes, but we heard Ruthie Joan; and she's with someone, so we didn't think you'd kidnapped two folks."

"We've wasted valuable time. What do you want us to do? Should we drive back to town and get a posse?" Willie asked.

"No. Follow me maybe you two could pull the beam out of the way and rescue Ruthie Joan and whoever's with her. Jessica and Robyn aren't strong enough to move it. I know my way around the woods, but I'd never go in the mine by myself," Amber replied, sort of like an after thought.

"Thought ya said somebody was with, uh, what's the little girl's name?"

"Ruthie Joan."

"Yes, yes, Ruthie Joan."

"I didn't hear anyone, but I guess there is. A boy."

"A boy?"

"Uh huh. She kept saying 'he'."

"Oh? How old is your friend?"

"Real old. Sixteen almost." Jeb and Willie smiled to themselves as they picked up their fishing poles and put them in the back of the truck. They picked up their bedrolls and kicked dirt and poured stale coffee onto the fire. They gave the campsite one last look, then they walked over to the truck.

"We need to walk. The road's too narrow on this side for the truck to make it," Amber said, walking back to the stand of trees where she exited the forest.

"Okay, walkin' it is. How far?"

"Not far. Ten minutes if we run."

"How far if we walk?" Willie asked, perspiration forming on his slightly unshaven upper lip.

"Twenty minutes, maybe half an hour."

"Then we better get started," Jeb said.

♠

CRASH BOOM CRASH

"What was that?" Willie asked, stopping in his tracks. He leaned against a tree. They'd left camp fifteen minutes earlier.

"I don't know, but it came from St. Gabriel's," Amber replied. Fear made her voice sound like a soft bass.

The three of them ran side by side and made it to the front of the mine. Jessica and Robyn were waiting outside. The entrance, was, once again, full of dust. Off to the side, partially hidden under a clump of fern, was evidence that Robyn had thrown up again.

"Another..." Jessica and Robyn began.

"Another beam or something fell."

"Is Ruthie Joan okay?" Amber asked.

"I... I don't know," Jessica answered. Robyn sat on the ground holding her stomach, said nothing.

"What's the girl's name again?" Jeb asked.

"Ruthie Joan," Robyn whispered.

"Ruthie Joan? Ruthie Joan? Can you hear me? I'm here with your friends. Can you hear me?" Jeb called, standing just inside the entrance. He pointed a dim flashlight into the dusty, black center.

"Willie, we can't move this rubble by ourselves. We need help." Willie searched the moist ground near the mine's entrance.

"Looks like only four folks been by here recently."

"What?" Jessica asked. She looked down at the ground next to Willie.

"Willie's an excellent tracker. Ma's Miwok. He can read signs good," Jeb replied as he ran his hands over the places Willie'd just run his.

"Somethin' wrong with one of 'em. Looks like they musta busted a leg. They're draggin it real bad. Musta made a splint or somethin' to help set it."

81

The Secret of St. Gabriel's Tower

"She's got polio," Robyn said, looking at the footprints. Ruthie Joan's dragging print, hers, Jessica and Amber's bare foot prints were clearly outlined in the moist soil close to and just inside the mine's entrance.

"Polio? I ain't going nowhere near polio," Jeb said, backing away from the girls.

"Really, Ruthie Joan can't hurt anyone. We go to school with her everyday, and no one's caught polio from her," Amber said, her face flushed with anger.

"No... no way I'm going near no polio," Jeb continued, quietly walking away from the girls.

"We're gonna need more help than these girls can give us," Willie said, as if Jeb hadn't spoken. The rumbling inside St. Gabriel's had ceased. The air around the opening cleared. Jeb stood his ground off to the side of the entrance and away from the girls.

"If you two can't help us, then I'll go get help," Amber said. "I'm wearing shoes, and I know my way to town."

"Yes. Maybe you should go. 'Course, folks are probably on their way here after all this noise," Willie replied.

"I don't think anyone will come 'cuz of the noise. We're use to hearing stuff coming from St. Gabriel's. That's why we're not suppose to play here," Robyn said.

"I better go. Folks'll believe one of the Triplets over strangers."

"Triplets? You girls don't look related," Willie looked from Jessica to Robyn to Amber and back to Jessica.

"We're not. We're friends. The town's folks call us that cuz we're always doing things together," Amber replied as she ran through the trees in the direction of town.

CHAPTER 8

"What's gotten into Amber?" A man asked, as he walked out of Matsuyama's general store. He and a number of other townspeople looked up Main toward the train station. Amber ran down the middle of the street right toward them.

"Look at that Walker girl, running through town like she owns it," an elderly man said to his checkers partner. They looked up from their game on the makeshift whiskey barrel table.

"Something must be wrong. It's not like one of the Triplets to run wild through the streets," replied another man following Amber's path through town.

"Maybe she found the Freeman girl. Them Triplets got special haunts. I swear they're not like regular girls," the first old man said.

"Miss Johnson, isn't that Amber?" Marie Beauregard asked. She patted her freshly pressed silver hair into place and rubbed invisible dust from her thick, black rimmed glasses.

The Secret of St. Gabriel's Tower

"Oh, what's wrong? Where's Jessica? They were together," Ruby Sue said, running out of her shop after Amber. "Amber... Amber...," Ruby Sue called. Amber continued running. She hadn't heard her. Mrs. Beauregard and Ruby Sue rushed outside, leaving the shop's front door wide open.

"Ruthie Joan and some man are trapped in St. Gabriel's Tower," Amber blurted out hysterically to those gathering in front of the Sheriff's office.

"Wait, now. Get your breath. What's this about Ruthie Joan? Have you seen Ruthie Joan?" Cal Robinson asked. He grabbed Amber, stopping her in her tracks. "Here, sit down," he said, guiding her to a wooden bench in front of City Hall.

"Uh huh, JJ, Robyn and a fisherman are trying to dig them out; but they need more help. The other fisherman's afraid of Ruthie Joan 'cuz of the polio. He's not helping at all," Amber said as she jumped up and pushed her way through the gathering crowd. She struggled to the Mayor's door.

"It's not like the Triplets to play a game about something this serious," a man said to his companion as they untied their horses and remounted for a trip to the mine.

"They'd never make up something about the mine," another person said.

"Daddy, daddy! Ruthie Joan's trapped in the mine, and JJ and Robyn are with her. And, uh...," Amber boomed. She fell on her hands and knees as Lincoln rushed outside to her cries. He opened the door just as she pushed from the other side. Two appraisers from Eureka, who'd been working with Lincoln, followed quickly behind him. The Sheriff arrived seconds later. Lincoln and the first appraiser lifted Amber to her feet. Her mouth worked, but no words came for a second.

"Amber, are you alright?" Lincoln asked, smothering her flushed and scratched face in his chest.

Safe in her father's arms, she began crying.

"That's okay, baby. You're safe. Now where are the others?" Lincoln asked. He wiped her face with a clean handkerchief and kissed her forehead.

"What's this about Jessica? You say she's trapped in the mine?" Ruby Sue exclaimed. She pushed her way between Linc and Amber. She had heard only the last few words of Amber's statement clearly.

"My baby! My baby! Sheriff, Linc. You have to do something. My baby's trapped in the mine." Ruby Sue pushed Amber away and grabbed the Sheriff by the front of his shirt. She pulled him to her as if he weighted ten pounds.

"Now, now, Ruby Sue, let go. Let's listen to what Amber has to say."

"But my baby..."

"Amber, where are the other girls?" the Sheriff asked, as calmly as he could with Ruby Sue tugging on one sleeve and Marie Beauregard on the other.

Amber gulped for air and said, "Ruthie Joan's trapped in the mine with some man; and JJ, Robyn and two strangers are trying to pull the wood off the entrance. I think part of the roof musta fell in. They're all in St. Gabriel's Tower."

"Oh my Lord, *in* St. Gabriel's tower. My baby, my baby," Ruby Sue screamed, falling back into the arms to Marie Beauregard and Sam Peterson.

"Here give her some water," Toshio Matsuyama said, handing a tin cup of cool water to Marie.

"Here, Ruby Sue, drink this."

"St. Gabriel's? How'd you think to look in there?" Linc asked. He held Amber close to his side as they walked outside.

Amber's voice muffled by her face buried in her father's chest, "we... we uh... we uh go there sometimes."

"You go there sometimes? And we were on the north side of the town," Linc said, as if speaking to himself, continuing to hold her close.

"Daddy we gotta go back. Hurry," Amber said, pulling away from her father's embrace. She was on the verge of tears.

"Don't worry honey. We'll get to Ruthie Joan and your friends," he answered.

The Secret of St. Gabriel's Tower

"Linc's right. Mount up men. We'll need the horses if we're going to St. Gab's; Buddy, hitch up your wagon. If Ruthie Joan's hurt, we may need it. Doc. Calvin, you better ride up front with Linc and me," Sheriff Brown said, mounting Red Ranger and leading ten mounted men out of town.

"Salley Jo, call Mable Louise. Tell her Amber's with me and that she's okay. Let her know that Ruthie Joan may be in St. Gabriel's," Linc yelled as Salley Jo rushed back into her office. Someone handed Linc a fresh horse. He lifted Amber up and sat her behind him and raced after the Sheriff.

"Sam, you go get Mrs. Freeman and Teddy if you can find him. If Ruthie Joan's hurt she's gonna need her family," the Sheriff shouted. Ruby Sue and Marie climbed in the back of Buddy's wagon. Ethelene threw blankets in after them and ran toward the train station.

"Homer, let David watch the station. Robyn's up in St. Gabriel's."

"What? St. Gabriel's! What's she doing there?" Homer asked, as he put a large manila package (from Amsterdam) in Issac Washington's mail slot. Not waiting for his wife's answer, he threw his black cotton postmaster apron toward David Adams and ran outside after Ethelene. Teddy and Mary Freeman picked them up in a second wagon.

"The road's too narrow for automobiles. But these wagons can travel off the road," someone in a wagon said, as if speaking the words out loud would make the travel shorter. Mrs. Freeman was seated in the back of the wagon with Ethelene and Homer. It rumbled behind the one carrying Ruby Sue and Marie. All were quiet, deep in their own personal thoughts.

"If she's okay, I'll kill her," Ruby Sue said between tears. She fingered a gold locket, opened it, and looked at a small shock of bright red hair.

"They're okay. They have to be okay," Ethelene, her face a mask of worry, fingered her rosary.

"Ethelene, where are the boys?" Ruby Sue shouted, above the horse and wagon noises. She looked around as if seeing Ethelene, Homer and Marie for the first time.

"Mable Louise's baby sitting. Oh, my goodness, Mable Louise. No one's told her about Amber."

"I'm sure someone's told her what Amber's told the rest of us. She'll be worried sick until we return. But at least she knows that her daughter's okay," Marie replied, patting Ruby Sue's hand.

"I'm glad the boys can't see us now. They're too young to understand why we're upset. They worship their sister. If anything's happen to her...;" Ethelene said, softly continuing to say her rosary while Homer prayed quietly at her side.

"Nothing's happened to her or to Jessica," Marie said as she unconsciously twisted a plain cotton handkerchief in her hand.

"Who are you?" Sheriff Brown asked Jeb, as the man walked out of the bushes not far from the old front entrance of St. Gabriel's. His movement startled the lead horse.

"He's okay, Sheriff. He's helping get Ruthie Joan out," Amber answered.

"Hello, Mr. Dixon, this is Sheriff Brown and my father, Mayor Walker," she continued as the men reined up the horses.

"Sheriff, Mayor," Jeb said, removing his hat and wiping sweat from his face and neck with his shirtsleeve. He extended his hand to the Sheriff and Lincoln.

"We'll need all your help. It looks as if the major supporting beam has rotted through and fallen across the entrance."

"Where's the other girls?" Linc asked, shaking Jeb's hand.

"Sitting outside on a log, near the side entrance. My fishing buddy, Willie Boyd's with 'em."

"Side entrance?" Sheriff Brown asked.

"What side entrance?" Linc echoed.

The Secret of St. Gabriel's Tower

"Are the girls okay?" Deputy Blake asked, riding up behind the foursome.

"Think so. Edwain, leave the horses here. We have to go to a side entrance."

"What side entrance?" The answer was drowned out by the arrival of the wagons.

"Where's my daughter?" Homer shouted. He jumped down from the first wagon before Teddy could stop. He grabbed Jeb by the front of his shirt.

"Homer, let him go. He's trying to help. Homer.., I said let him go," Sheriff Brown yelled, taking Homer's hands and removing them from the front of Jeb's shirt.

"I understand. I'd react the same way if it were my daughter lost. She's over there," Jeb said, pointing through a thicket of tangled bushes to the side of St. Gabriel's'.

"Over there? I don't see anything," Linc said.

"Daddy, Mayor, over here," Jessica answered, from the other side of the thicket.

"Keep talking, honey. I can't see you," Linc replied. He ran after Homer who, rushing through the brushes toward the sound of Jessica's voice, was moving faster than anyone'd seen since his old baseball days.

"Robyn, Robyn, baby, are you okay?"

"I'm okay, daddy," Robyn said, her voice raw with emotion.

Robyn ran toward her father. They hugged. She took his hand and drug him to where Jessica and Willie stood. "Oh daddy, I'm so scared! I think she may be dead. We haven't heard her since the last beam fell. She's in there with someone." Robyn's words ran together. She clung to her father's arm. Her face was ashen and her teeth chattered.

"We'll get her out. Robyn, I know you're scared. I'm scared too. But I need my arm back if I'm going to help move this timber," Homer said softly. He gently removed Robyn hand from his. The rest of the town arrived and began moving fallen rocks while he spoke.

"Mom. Mom, are you alright?" Jessica asked, looking into her mother's stricken face.

"Jessica, you... I'm so glad you're okay," Ruby Sue replied, taking Jessica's face in her hands and kissing her cheeks. "I thought... I thought... we'll talk later. I'm going to help rescue Ruthie Joan." She gave Jessica another hug. Then she picked up a shovel from the ground where Buddy had placed them and began shoveling dirt from the entrance.

"Robyn, come here and stay out of the way," Ethelene said.

"But, Mama, I want to help."

"You can help by staying out of everyone's way," Ethelene said. She gave Robyn an extra squeeze and joined Ruby Sue.

"Ruthie Joan?" Sheriff Brown called loudly, causing loose dirt to fall from the top of the entrance.

"Ruthie Joan?" he called in a softer tone. More dirt fell. He walked outside and held up his hands for quiet. "We have to be careful. It's very unstable in there. The slightest noise causes the ceiling to crumble."

"Oh no, Ruthie Joan!" Mrs. Freeman cried. She tried to run past him to the mine.

"Edwain, Homer, one of you take Mrs. Freeman to the wagons over there." He pointed to where Teddy's wagon and horses stood. Sheriff Brown walked over to where the rest of the townspeople stood.

"We have to be very careful. The mine is unstable, and we don't want anyone hurt. Especially not anyone in the mine. Okay?"

"Okay," Buddy said gently slapped a pick ax handle in his right hand. Others in the crowd nodded.

The Secret of St. Gabriel's Tower

"Buddy, you take a few men and see if the main entrance is any more stable than this," Sheriff Brown directed.

"No. Don't go in there. We haven't been in there since we were nine. The main entrance is full of boulders," cried Amber.

Robyn broke away from her mother and ran to stand next to Jessica and Amber. She said, "JJ's right. The main entrance is very dangerous. Someone might get smashed by a falling rock."

"Thank you, girls, but I'll see for myself," Buddy replied. He walked back through the trees toward the main entrance. Six men followed him.

"Okay, men follow me. Remember, you must be as quiet as possible. We don't want a cave-in. Ethelene, you and Ruby Sue go see about Mrs. Freeman and send Deputy Blake back."

"But, Sheriff," Ethelene protested.

"We'll talk about it later. I need some strong men to help move these rocks, and we'd better hurry. It'll be dark in a coupla hours, and I don't think anyone thought to bring flashlights."

"Willie and me have a flashlight somewhere around here," Jeb said, as he looked near the boulder by the side entrance. "Ah, here it is." He picked up the flashlight and flicked the switch then turned it to the ground. The light dimly lit the grass.

He hit the flashlight on his knee and flicked the switch again. He smiled. The light shown brightly for a second, then faded. "Darn, the batteries won't last much longer. Willie, Willie, did you bring your flashlight?"

"Uh huh. I thought you were afraid of the polio," Willie whispered.

"I am. But these folks don't seem to be."

"The flashlight's over near the guns. Want me to go get it?" Willie asked, loud enough for the Sheriff to hear him.

"Yes, if you don't mind. We're going to need light, and it will take too long to go back to town," Sheriff Brown replied.

"Mary, you better sit down. You don't look to well. You have to take care of yourself in your condition," Ethelene said. She wet a handkerchief with water from one of the wagon canteens and patted Mrs. Freeman's forehead.

94

Mrs. Freeman did not reply. She sat wrapped in a black wool coat. Her teeth chattered. Her face was waxen.

"Doc. Doc Calvin, you'd better look after Mary. She don't ... she doesn't look too good," Ethelene said.

"I gave her something in the wagon just as we arrived. She'll be okay. It's pretty mild, with her pregnancy and all. She'll sleep as soon as she sees Ruthie Joan," Doc Calvin said. He took Mrs. Freeman's pulse. "Here, Mary. Sit down next to his wagon wheel."

"It's okay for her to remain here. She needs to hear folks working to free Ruthie Joan."

"Ma, Ma? I'm goin' wit' Buddy," Teddy shouted. He ran after Buddy Shaw's retreating figure.

"Teddy?"

"He's okay. He's with Buddy," Ethelene said.

♠

"Well, I'll be," Buddy said. He held a small stub of candle in his right hand. He entered a mine opening which was barely big enough to allow him passage. On the far side of the old entrance, as the girls had said, the opening was completely blocked with old and recent boulders.

"Teddy, go git the others. Looks like we may be able to git in this way. Hurry. I don't have much light. Have 'em bring flashlights." Buddy held the candle high above his head. He shaded his eyes as the large cavernous space burst into color when his candlelight hit the walls.

"I'll be," he repeated. A few minutes later, Teddy, followed by the rest of posse stood beside Buddy. Willie returned with a flashlight.

"Did you find Ruthie Joan?" Robyn asked. She pushed her way past the adults and peered into the darkened opening.

"No, but I found a way in. Anyone bring a flashlight?"

"Here," Sheriff Brown said, taking one of the flashlights from Willie. He followed Buddy to the opening.

"Oh, my goodness. Has this been here all this time?" Homer Jones asked, staring open mouthed at the beautiful sight before them.

"Guess so. Never knew about this place," Buddy replied.

"Guess we better go inside and look around. Maybe there's a way to get to Ruthie Joan from here," Sheriff Brown said, stepping deeper into the multicolored cave.

"Whatcha looking at?" Amber asked. She reached the cave entrance as the last of the men entered. Robyn and Jessica waited outside.

"This looks like the lepidolite crystal caves we have back home," Jeb said, to no one in particular.

"Looks like Buddy found a cave much more beautiful than our secret place."

"Well, are we going in? We're the ones who found Ruthie Joan, and we should get the credit," Amber said, walking past Jessica.

"Of course we're going in. I just wish I'd brought shoes like you. If I step on a slug, I know I'm going to wet my pants," Robyn said. She took a deep breath, shuddered and then followed Amber.

"You're not going to leave me out here," Jessica said as she stepped gingerly on the damp soil. The other girls were right in front of her. The lights from the men's flashlights sparkled on the pink, green, brown and yellow walls of the mine.

"Wow. This is beautiful. No wonder Ruthie Joan came in here. I'd follow someone in here to see this," Amber said, her voice echoing off the walls to the scurrying sound of bats.

"Bats. How'd they get in here? We've never seen bats in our mine."

"This must be another mine. Maybe it's connected to ours." Robyn ran her hands over the smooth glass-like wall surface and looked around in awe.

Patricia E. Canterbury

"Girls, if you're coming with us, you have to keep up. I don't like the idea of you girls being in here. But I know I can't keep you out. So keep close. I don't want anyone falling behind," Deputy Blake said. "Keep up. And don't go wandering off into any of those adjacent openings."

"How do you know where to go?" Amber asked.

"Look, you can see Ruthie Joan's footprints and those of someone else," Deputy Blake said as he pointed his flashlight on the mine floor. One set of footprints stood out from the rest, that of feet dragging and prints deep in the soil like something was heavy on the legs.

"Let us have one of the flashlights back here."

"You can have this candle. We don't have enough flashlights to go around," one of the posse said.

"Thanks!" Jessica took the almost whole candle from him.

"I wonder who she's with," Robyn said.

"Who'd take her in a mine? Maybe, he was going to kill her, Or maybe keep her in here and ask her folks for money," Amber said.

"Her folks don't have any money."

"Maybe he didn't know that."

"*Yesth*, maybe."

"What are you girls talking about back there? Come here and walk in the middle. I don't want to have to send a posse after the three of you. You should have stayed with the women," Deputy Blake said.

"Why would we stay with the women? We're not afraid of the dark or any old stupid mine. Besides, we're the ones who found Ruthie Joan. We're going to be the ones to save her too," Amber whispered. Her whisper was heard by the entire group.

"Sheriff, I'll talk to her once we get Ruthie Joan. Do you think it's safe to call to her?" Lincoln asked, looking past the crowd to his daughter.

"I'm sorry. I just said what I was thinking," Amber said, answering her father's unasked question. The posse stopped walking.

97

"What's the matter? Why are we stopping?"

"Looks like a cave-in. We can't go any further," Sheriff Brown said.

"Cave-in looks old. We must have taken a wrong turn," Homer Jones said.

"Their footprints are all around here. They came this way."

"We have to back track."

"Keep an eye open for more prints."

"Maybe we should break up and go looking in the other tunnels," Amber said a she turned toward a tunnel to her left.

"I'm not going anywhere by myself," Jessica whispered.

"Me either. Besides, Deputy Blake said we had to stay together," Robyn replied.

"We can go together. Let's stay here until the posse passes by. Then we'll go another way," Amber whispered.

"What if we get lost?"

"We won't. We'll just follow our footsteps back the way we came."

Keeping back for a few minutes until the light from the posse dimmed, the Triplets walked into the right tunnel opposite the one taken by the posse.

"We're not getting anywhere but lost. Amber, we've been to three dead-ends," Robin continued.

"I know she's on the other side of one of these. She's gotta be. Look, her footprints came this way. So did the man she's with."

"It looks like she's sightseeing," Jessica looked down at the latest set of prints going in every direction leading to a new entrance.

"It doesn't look like she's being dragged in here," Robyn said, staring into the bright light reflecting from the walls.

"What is this stuff?" Amber asked, "It sure is pretty." She marveled at the stunning colors the candlelight brought out.

"I don't know. I bet that we could sell tickets and have folks pay to see this. It's really beautiful."

"Amber, Jessica, come quick, look at this wall. It musta just fallen in," Robyn shouted. She rushed to a pile of fresh, loose dirt and rocks directly in front of them.

"Help, is there somebody there?" A female voice from the other side of the slide asked.

"Ruthie Joan? Is that you?" Robyn asked.

"Yes, who's there? I can't see. It's so dark." Ruthie Joan's voice, edged with fright, was high and barely discernable.

"It's us, the Triplets, again. We're on the other side of the rocks. A town posse's with us."

"Posse?" Ruthie Joan sobbed.

"Uh huh. They came looking for you."

"For me? Am I going to die? You can't get me out," Ruthie Joan's words were muffled between sobs.

"Uh huh, 'cuz you've been kidnapped," Amber said, her voice causing a few loose rocks to tumble to the floor.

"Careful, you'll have the whole place cave in on us," Jessica said, speaking over Ruthie Joan's words. She pressed her ear against the wall.

"What did you say?" Robyn asked, "We couldn't hear."

"I said, uh... no I wasn't. Uh... I came t' see the walls. Walter's uh... hurt though. I think h's... h's leg's broke. He uh... lost a lot of blood."

"Walter? Who's Walter?" Robyn asked, turning toward Amber and Jessica who shrugged. The girls began pulling at the rocks as the Sheriff and others caught up with them.

"We came lookin' for you girls. Whatcha doin'?" Deputy Blake asked.

"Ruthie Joan's in there," Jessica pointed to the rockslide.

"Girls, move away from the rocks," Sheriff Brown said.

"Ruthie Joan are you okay?" He shouted.

"Yes," a nearly hysterical voice replied.

"Can you move away from the rocks?"

"Uh huh. Please hurry. It's dark in here."

"Good, move as far away as you can. We're going to start digging at this end."

The Secret of St. Gabriel's Tower

"Okay. Ma? Ma? Is Ma with you? Ma?"

"Yes, your mother's just outside. You'll be able to see her very soon," the Sheriff said. To Lincoln Walker he said "Get Mary. Maybe the sound of her voice will comfort the girl."

"Sheriff, I don't think Mary should be down here. The excitement may be too much for her in her condition," Doc Calvin said. "Better have Teddy talk to her if need be."

"You're right. Teddy, come here keep talking to your sister. Your voice might calm her when the diggin' gets heavy."

"Okay." Teddy knelt down on one knee and whispered, "Ruthie Joan, are you okay? Can you hear me?"

"Uh huh. Teddy, I'm scared. It's dark and he's not breathin'," she whimpered.

"I'm right here. Ma's jest outside."

During the next couple of hours, rocks and dirt were moved to a connecting tunnel immediately to the right of where the girls found Ruthie Joan. Suddenly, the wall broke open; and Sheriff Brown touched one of Ruthie Joan's braces.

"I got her!" he shouted. "I need someone to crawl in and help push her out."

"I'll go," Jeb said. "I'm skinny. I can crawl in there and push her out."

"What 'bout the polio?" Willie asked.

"What 'bout it? There's a little girl trapped in there. None of these folks seem scared of getting it. Maybe I won't be either."

♠

Jeb crawled through the small opening. It was pitch black for a few minutes then his eyes became accustom to the darkness but he still couldn't see very far. "Ruthie Joan, where are you? Say something so I can locate you."

"I... I'm right here," Ruthie Joan's voice sounded very close.

100

"Keep talking Ruthie Joan, I'll get you." Jeb crawled forward a few yards and bumped into Ruthie Joan's braced leg. He shuddered for a second and tried to stand up. There was enough headroom for him to stand fully upright. He said, "come on, Ruthie Joan, I'm right here. I'll help you up." He put his arm around her waist and helped her back the way he'd come in. The posse continued digging and the opening was now big enough for a full-size man to enter.

Blinking from the flashlights' glare and the reflections from the rocks, Ruthie Joan held on to Jeb. Her dress was splattered with dirt, mud, dust and dried blood.

Teddy gathered her up in his arms and carried her out to the light.

"Let me look at her," Doc Calvin said. He felt her forehead. Then he took out his stethoscope and listened to her heart beat. "Seems okay. Hand me a blanket. This won't hurt a bit," he said, giving her a shot in the arm.

"I'm alright now that I can see. It was scary in there. I couldn't hardly breath. Please look at Walter. I don't think he's breathing," she repeated. Her teeth chattered. She pulled the blanket closer to her body.

"Everyone, you better stay here," Sheriff Brown said. He took out gun. "Deputy Blake, follow me."

Deputy Blake reappeared a minute later. "Men, bring another blanket. We have to carry him out."

Walter lay on his back on the floor of the cave where Jeb had just removed Ruthie Joan. A medium size boulder lay across his legs. Deputy Blake pushed the boulder off the injured young man. Homer threw a blanket over him. They rolled him onto a makeshift stretcher and carried him out to where the posse waited.

"Let me look at him," Doc Calvin said. He opened the young man's eyelids. He listened to his shallow breathing. He took out a pair of scissors and cut away the bloody right pant leg.

"Looks like his leg's broken. Compound fracture from the look of it. He's lost a lot of blood, but he'll be okay. Someone get me some tree limbs for a splint. Some of you men take hold of this blanket and take him outside."

"Will we be able to get him through the cave's opening?" someone asked.

"Yes, we've already widened it enough to take him through," someone else replied.

"Why, that's the Williams' boy. His folks live over in Grants Cove," Paul Barton said, looking down at the unconscious young man.

"His name's Walter. He's my friend. And, uh, he ain't 'fraid of polio, like some. He said he knew of some really pretty tunnels that were prettier than them in the books. And, uh, he said he never told nobody 'bout his mines. And uh, I was the first t' see it. We walked around to see all the different colors," Ruthie Joan said.

"I fell over there. He came t' get me and the roof fell in trapped us. And, uh, we thought we're going back to other way we come, and, uh, we come thisa way," she said as she pointed to the dark tunnel that had been her home for the past 25 hours.

"The matches burned out; and, uh, we kept walking. Then, uh, then, uh, the board fell on Walter and I tried dragging him out 'cuz I seen a light and went outside only I was lost. And uh I come back for him when the roof fell in for good. Walter was caught under things. I, uh, I couldn't lift him. He was nice. I didn't think no one would find us," she said, as she clung to her brother.

"The shot I gave her is taking effect. She'll be asleep soon," Doc Calvin said. He felt her forehead again before Teddy picked her up and carried her outside.

♠

The ride back to town was quiet except for Mary Freeman's soft cries as she patted Ruthie Joan's right hand. Teddy, seated next to his mother, held Ruthie Joan's left. Ruthie Joan and Walter

Williams lay side by side wrapped in woolen blankets in the bottom of Teddy's wagon. Sam Peterson drove the team of horses. Ruby Sue, Marie and the Triplets rode in Buddy's wagon. Four men carried the two young people to the four-bed hospital at the rear of Doc Calvin's office.

CHAPTER 11

"Sheriff, how'd Ruthie Joan's ribbon get in my room?" Ned asked, as Sheriff Brown unlocked the cell.

"We don't really know. Ruthie Joan said she noticed it missing right after she and Walter passed by Ridge Road."

"That's right by my place."

"Yep. We figured that Wally, your pet raccoon, must a taken it. We found it right near his food, if you remember. I didn't stop to think that *he* might have found it outside. I'm really sorry I doubted you."

"I'm just glad she's okay. I couldn't imagine that somebody actually took her," Ned replied. He shuddered, picked up his jacket and book and walked outside.

"Afternoon, Ned, beautiful day isn't it?" Sam Peterson said, as he walked past him on Main Street.

"Afternoon, yep beautiful. Cooling off, too," Ned replied, inhaling the fresh fog laden salt air.

♠

"Teddy, you can take your mother and sister home," Doc Calvin said. Mary and Ruthie Joan were already seated in the back of Deputy Blake's black Ford.

"They'll both be okay. Your mom's fine. And Ruthie Joan just has a few scratches. Buddy's repairing her bent leg brace. He'll bring it round tomorrow. I'll send Laurel over to check on them both later today, and I'll come by tomorrow. You take these pills when you get home. It'll help you sleep. Mrs. Wilson'll keep the little ones for a few days. I sent word to Theodore that everything's okay. No use in him worrying about his family. The town'll take care of what needs taken care of. Now get."

♠

"Mom, dad, it was so exciting. We found Ruthie Joan and her friend and this beautiful cave; and, ah, can we go there after supper?" Jessica, eating a bowl of chicken soup, looked from one anxious parent to the other as they checked her over and over.

"Ruby Sue, shouldn't she be laying down?" Jimmy John asked, looking at Jessica's red face and bright eyes.

"JJ, do you feel okay?" Ruby Sue asked, feeling her forehead for the hundredth time since they arrived back in their home.

"Uh huh. I feel fine. Just a little sunburn. I forgot to take my hat with me. But the fog's coming in. Tomorrow it'll be cool."

"I think you should lay down for an hour," Jimmy John said.

"I'm not tired."

"I think you should lay down," he stated, firmly.

"Okay, but I'm not going to sleep," she replied, yawning and scratching her sunburned cheeks.

♠

"Where's Robyn? Is she with the boys?" Homer asked, walking into the kitchen where Ethelene was chipping pieces of ice off the block.

"She's in the boy's room. She's been with them ever since we came home. Take this ice water in for her. Her stomach was really upset and her cheeks were flushed a few minutes ago."

Homer returned to the kitchen and handed the glass of ice water back to Ethelene. "She's sound asleep on the floor between the boy's beds. I guess she's not as grown up as she likes to believe. We might as well let her rest.

♠

"Mother, you have to come with daddy and me and see the cave. It's full of these really beautiful tunnels. Mr. Peterson said they are mica caves. He said that the mica comes in really great colors like gray, green or brown. Some are black. I didn't see any of those. We say lep ... the lep-id-o-lite...," Amber pronounced the word slowly.

"The lepidolite caves are full of pink and green and light brown and yellow mica. All the time we were playing in St. Gabriel's we didn't know it had this really beautiful side. Daddy said Ruthie Joan and Walter discovered a totally new cave that's full of minerals that will help the town," she continued, her voice was filled with excitement.

"Amber you, should rest. You've had enough excitement to last all summer. First you climb to the top of the Main Street

The Secret of St. Gabriel's Tower

Tower, then you find Ruthie Joan and go gallivanting through caves. My, my, you have all summer to find troubles. I want you to take a nap."

"I'm too excited to sleep. Besides, naps are for little kids," Amber replied, yawning in spite of herself.

"Uh huh. Well, if you're not going to lay down, you can come outside and sit with me while I weed the vegetables. We want to make sure we have enough to bring to the Anderson's party. We can't let the jack rabbits get them all," Mable Louise said. She looked over at Amber just as she stifled another yawn.

"Mother, I'm so happy that Mr. Dixon finally went in the cave and helped pull Ruthie Joan out. I was so angry at him when he said he was afraid of Ruthie Joan's polio. No one's caught polio from her."

"I know, dear. We have to be thankful that he overcame his fear. He was the only adult small enough to reach her."

CHAPTER 12

"Ruthie Joan, are you sure that you're up to this?" Caroline Anderson asked. She handed a starched white damask tablecloth and table netting to Ruthie Joan. Caroline's tall, slender figure momentarily blocked Ruthie Joan's view of the tables. Tucking an errant strand of blue black hair into the pale yellow knit netting surround her long hair, Caroline waited for Ruthie Joan's reply.

"Yes, Miz Anderson. My legs get a little weak. But if I set down ever so often, I be okay. Ma and me are real glad to help out," Ruthie Joan replied. She limped to the long wooden banquet tables the farm hands placed under the grove of redwood trees on the Anderson's back lawn. Ruthie Joan spread the tablecloths on the table pads then placed the silverware in the carefully arranged order specified by Daisy Martine, the Anderson's housekeeper.

"Now how's it go? Oh yeah, first you put the rolled rectanglar napkins in the center of the plate," Ruthie Joan said. She put a china plate and napkin on the first of 50 tables.

The Secret of St. Gabriel's Tower

"Good, plate and napkin. Then uh... two forks, one for dinner at far left and one for dessert just left of plate. Put the knife next to the plate to the right, two spoons, dessert to right of knife and soup spoon to far right. Butter plate, water glass and ashtrays to the top of plate," Ruthie Joan continued speaking to herself. She wiped off the spotless heavy silver and crystal ashtrays and then stepped back to admire the place setting.

"Everything looks fine, Ruthie Joan. You better sit down for a while I don't want you getting faint," Daisy Martine, a reed-thin, narrow mouthed light skinned woman said.

"I be alright. Fog's comin' in."

"I don't want anything more to happen to you," Daisy said, as she set the second place in the exact duplicate of Ruthie Joan's.

♠

Mary Freeman poured fresh squeezed lemonade into one of the many wooden buckets next to a stack of crystal cups on the kitchen table. She tasted the lemonade, "This be okay. Betterin' mine. Ned, take these out to them tables over yonder where Ruthie Joan be."

"Okay." Ned picked up the buckets of lemonade and placed them in the shade next to the tables. He set them next to the four crystal serving bowls he'd put on the table earlier.

"Hello, Mr. Simon. I... I'm sorry you got in trouble 'cuz of me," Ruthie Joan stammered. She looked him squarely in the face.

"Don't matter none. Folks here are real nice. They admit when they make a mistake. The Sheriff and Deputy haven't treated me any differently 'cuz of what they thought I'd done. I still get odd jobs from folks. I still work for the Johnson's, and Mr. Barton has me diggin' graves in the cemetery whenever Junior Montgomery can't," Ned replied. He blushed almost as much as Ruthie Joan.

"We better hurry, folks be arriving already," Ruthie Joan said. She put the last place setting on the last table just as the first line of cars, horses and buggies began coming up the main road.

♠

"Gosh, I keep forgetting how beautiful the Anderson's house is," Amber said. She looked out the car window toward a large sprawling three-story redwood-sided farmhouse. The house was the largest in the TriCove area. The household help consisted of five live-ins, plus sixty or so farm hands who tended the cattle and sheep over the 3,000 acres north and east of The Coves. Ten more employees worked on the two salmon trawlers moored at Grant's Cove.

"It is impressive. We're lucky to have such generous folks in the Coves. Never put on airs, just regular folks like everyone else," Lincoln said. He struggled to keep the car in the middle of the horse and buggy rut filled dirt road.

"Yes, just regular folks," Mable Louise echoed. Lincoln parked the car next to the first row of parked cars.

"Hi, Teddy. It sure smells wonderful. You can smell the bar-be-que all the way to Holland's Reef Road," Amber said. She handed Teddy two baskets of vegetables when he opened the rear door of her family's car.

"Yep. My mouth's been waterin' all morning."

"How's Ruthie Joan?" Mable Louise asked as Teddy helped her from the car.

"She's fine. She be over yonder." He pointed toward the rows of tables, and waved at a distant figure. The figure, dressed in a long pale yellow dress covered by a white eyelet apron, waved back. "Ma's helping in the kitchen. The little ones are playing over yonder." This time he pointed behind the great house where the laughter of children filled the air.

111

The Secret of St. Gabriel's Tower

"All the children are here?" Amber asked, following to a near by table. She handed an armload of wild flowers in a large blue glass vase to Daisy.

"Yep. Them, the Jones' boys, and a bunch of Anderson cousins are playing like old friends," he replied. They listened for a minute to the children's play.

♠

"Welcome one and all. Caroline ...," John Anderson gestured to his wife who was seated next to him at the head table."Danny ...," he gestured to the table where his son sat with the Triplets and other young teens, "and I are honored to have you attend our Juneteenth celebration. The celebration has special meaning this year because one of our own was found safe after being lost for over a day."

"Amen," Some in the crowd said.

"Walter Williams is also with us. I see, son, that your leg is getting better." John Anderson, a tall, dark, big boned man said. He spoke into a megaphone so the four hundred or so guests could hear him clearly. Walter, seated with the Triplets, nodded to the smiling faces of those around him.

"Let's eat and drink before I tell you great tales of Juneteenth," John Anderson said. "Reverend Clark, a prayer." The Reverend stood and said a blessing for the food. John looked around at the tables spread out over the back lawn filled to overflowing with foods of all types. "Amen."

"Folks worked all morning making sure the food was just right, dig in. We have something here for everyone, early summer corn on the cob from the Matsuyama farm. Thanks Toshio."

Toshio stood up to the applause. He bowed to the Andersons and resumed his seat next to his wife, Michiko. Michiko, recently arrived from Kyoto, Japan, was attending her first barbecue.

"The steaks are from our own cattle, and the ribs are from Henry du Pree's pigs. Thanks, Henry."

"No trouble at all. If you want good ribs, come to me," he said. He waved at the crowd and helped himself to an extra serving of potato salad.

"Eat hearty, remember to leave room for desert. Rachel Wilson's made her famous peach cobbler. Now, I know there's not enough of that to go around because I'm havin' the first helping. There's homemade strawberry ice cream and Daisy's Dutch marble cake. I'm havin' firsts on them also," John laughed.

"Now you know why we have such a big place. It's to keep John in *vittles*," Caroline joked.

"She's right. Eat up. I'll tell you about Juneteenth during dessert. The baseball game between Poplar Cove and Grant's Cove will begin an hour after dessert over near the main gate. Square dancing's in the barn starts about eight. That should just about make it a day," John sat down and gave his wife a kiss on the cheek.

As the house staff and farm hands cleared the main supper dishes, John Anderson, stood up, cigar in hand and said, "For those who are new to the Coves, and who aren't from Texas, let me tell you the truth about one of the most honored holidays from back home." He cleared his throat and took a sip of lemonade.

"General Gordon Granger landed with federal troops in Galveston. Galveston's a small little town just a short way from where my family's from." Everyone laughed. "General Granger with the expressed mission of forcing slave owners to release their slaves. This happened on June 19, 1865. This was, as all of you know, over two years after Lincoln announced the Emancipation Proclamation. Some of you've heard that it took two years because slave owners held up the news to have one more crop; or those of you from Oklahoma heard the story of the Negro ex-Union solider who rode his mule all the way cross country carrying the message from President Lincoln, himself, that the slaves were free. Oklahomans like to tell the story that it was on June 19, 1865, that he arrived in Oklahoma. But we Texans know that it was Old

113

The Secret of St. Gabriel's Tower

General Granger who told the tale, least wise, that's the Texas version; and I'm sticking to it. Ever since, June 19th has been celebrated just as we will today with family and friends, good food, a baseball game or two, and dancing under the stars. Ah, here's dessert, eat up and go root for our boys to beat the stuffing out of Grant's Cove."

"This is a little different from the way you told it," Lewis Jackson said, as he turned toward Issac Washington.

"It's his celebration. I was speakin' from memory. Everything else we talked about is correct. You'll find out when we have a moment alone with Anderson. We'll have cigars in the library when the dancing begins in an hour."

"Are you sure that he's going to help?" Lewis asked, looking sideways in John Anderson's direction.

"He's a smart business man. He has lots of stock. He knows a gold mine when he sees it. Mark my words, in a couple years, 1929 or '30, right before Thanksgiving, we'll be rich beyond our wildest dreams," Issac Washington whispered. He lit a hand rolled Havana cigar.

"I don't know if it's a good idea to spread ourselves so thin. I don't like dealing in speculations. Give me jewelry or gold coins, something I can put my hands on."

"The market's firm. Colored folks just getting a taste of what Astor and those folks back east been doing for years. This time next year I expect to be living in New York, going to the swell places that truly rich Negroes go," Issac said. He blew smoke into the gathering fog.

"You brought the jewel with you?" he continued.

"No, I don't carry something like that around with me. It's safe. I've got pictures." Lewis said.

"Whatya fellas so involved in?" Noah asked, as he got up and straightened his aching back.

"Lewis, I don't think you had much time to visit with Noah Sullivan. He's the editor of the Poplar Cove Tribune."

"Pleased t' meet you," Noah said. He wiped his hands off on one of the damask napkins, and extended his hand to Lewis.

"Lewis Jefferson, from Harlem," Issac said, smiling broadly.

"Harlem, huh? What brings you out west?" Noah asked.

"Visiting old friends. Looking at a few mines up north toward Lassen," Lewis replied. He narrowed his eyes and looked Noah over as if sizing him for a suit.

"Yep, we go way back," Issac said. He spooned a large helping of ice cream into a shallow bowl.

♠

"Robyn, Amber, who's that man talking to Mr. Washington?" Jessica asked. She looked past their table where they sat with Daniel Anderson, Three Shaw, Bobby Joe Allen and Walter, to the one with Bank president Washington, and his guest, Doc. Calvin, Henry DuPree, Noah Sullivan, and several land owners from Marshall and Grant's Cove.

"He must be really important. He's sitting with the really rich folks' table."

"Where?" Amber croaked, she squinted toward the tables.

"I don't know him. But he's the fella I told you I saw at the station the day we thought Ruthie Joan'd been kidnapped," Robyn replied. "Look, Mr. Thomas' with that same man we saw a few days ago. I wonder what he's doing here? Mark my words, something strange is going on at the bank."

"I don't see anyone," Amber said, again.

"You're going to have to tell your parents that you can't see very well. You're getting worse."

"I'm not going to wear ugly old glasses like Miss Beauregard," Amber countered.

"Okay with me if you can't see."

"I see just fine."

"Still, we better find out what's going on at the bank. Mr. Washington and Mr. Thomas are both doing some strange things. I saw Mr. Thomas talking to that same man over by Miss Ruby's dance place."

"It's really nice of the Anderson's to hire Ruthie Joan to do the starching and ironing during the summer," Amber said, changing the subject. "One of the farm hands is going to drop the laundry by the Freeman's on his way to the feed store. Mother said that Mrs. Blake is going to tutor Ruthie Joan during the summer. Ruthie Joan may be able to work for the Anderson's during other school breaks."

"*Yesth*. Mom said that the family really needs help, especially now that Mrs. Freeman's going to have another baby. Here comes Ruthie Joan now. Ruthie Joan, are you finished with your chores?"

"Uh huh. Oh, hi, Walter," Ruthie Joan said. She looked at Walter sitting at the end of the Triplets' table his right leg in a cast. His crutches lay beneath the table.

"Hi, Ruthie Joan," he replied, suddenly very interested in the pattern of the tablecloth.

"Ruthie Joan, come eat dessert with us."

"I guess I can."

"Then sit down with us. You can sit next to Walter," Amber said. She moved over to make room for her. The Triplets giggled as Ruthie Joan and Walter blushed.

"Did Walter tell you the news?" Ruthie Joan asked.

"No, what?" the Triplets asked, in unison, something they were doing more and more lately.

"Let me," Walter said.

"It seems the cave I ... we, Ruthie Joan and me, that we found. It's a new vein of mica. Our families can lay claim to it. We might make enough to go to college," he said, softly looking directly at Ruthie Joan who suddenly discovered an interesting pattern on her skirt.

"Wow! That's wonderful. Jimmy Wil loves college."

"Yes, that's wonderful. Ruthie Joan, we're so happy for you. You too Walter," Robyn and Amber said.

"Well, what are we going to do for excitement for the rest of the summer? We can't go finding new caves. We can't even go into St. Gabriel's since the townspeople sealed both of the old entrances," Amber said.

"I had enough excitement for the rest of the year," Ruthie Joan replied.

"Me too," Walter said.

"No one needs to worry. The Coves are pretty quiet," Three said. As he wiped syrup from the peach cobbler from his chin.

"I'm sure something will happen," Jessica and Robyn said, in unison.

"Yes, something like finding out what's someone from Harlem doing spending so much time with our town's banker," Amber said.

"Who are we talking about? Jessica asked, turning around and looking directly into the smiling face of Lewis Jackson.

"Him, mark my words. There'll be trouble before the summer's over and he'll be involved," Amber whispered.

"Nope, he harmless. We'll have to find adventure from someone else," Robyn said.

The End